We're Fa

'We're *what?*' Annie as

'Cousins-in-law?'

'Loose connections, at the very most,' she said repressively. '*Temporary* loose connections.'

On the wide front porch, Tucker turned and lifted a hand in careless salute. She watched him stride down the front path and wondered what there was about the man that made him so impossible to ignore.

Family?

No way. There was something going on here, but for the life of her, she couldn't figure out what it was. They weren't really family. On the other hand, they weren't really friends. Which left…

'Don't ask. Don't even think about it,' she muttered, and slammed the door hard enough to rattle the bevelled glass panels.

Dear Reader,

The summer sun's shining and that's perfect weather to settle down with these sensual love stories! Kick off your shoes, get yourself a long, cold drink and relax…

July's MAN OF THE MONTH is rugged and sexy Clark Garrison, but why exactly has he returned to town after all these years? Find out in Mary Lynn Baxter's *Heart of Texas*. Another man reappears from the past in Eileen Wilks's *Proposition: Marriage*—seductive spy Samuel Charmaneaux just *has* to rescue Jane Smith!

Barbara McCauley's powerful SECRETS! trilogy ends this month with *Killian's Passion*, where Cara Sinclair never expected to fall in love with the long-lost millionaire she was sent to find. And *he* never suspected he was a millionaire!

In *The Bride-in-Law* from the ever-popular Dixie Browning opposites attract! And Lexi Parker meets a man who sets her on fire in Shawna Delacorte's *The Daddy Search*.

And finally, we start a new trilogy this month. Cathie Linz's light-hearted MARRIAGE MAKERS series kicks off with *Too Sexy for Marriage*. Enjoy the fun with Jason Knight and Heather Grayson, and look out for the other Knight siblings coming in August and September.

Enjoy them all!

The Editors

The Bride-in-Law
DIXIE BROWNING

™SILHOUETTE
DESIRE®

Silhouette, Silhouette Desire and Colophon
are registered trademarks of Harlequin Books S.A.,
used under licence.

First published in Great Britain 2000
Silhouette Books, Eton House, 18-24 Paradise Road,
Richmond, Surrey TW9 1SR

© Dixie Browning 1999

ISBN 0 373 76251 8

22-0007

Printed and bound in Spain
by Litografia Rosés S.A., Barcelona

DIXIE BROWNING

has also written a number of historical romances with her sister under the name Bronwyn Williams. A member of Romance Writers of America, Dixie has won numerous awards for her work. She divides her time between Winston-Salem and the Outer Banks of North Carolina, USA.

One

***

The note was in the sugar bowl, where he'd be sure to find it. Tucker read it through, swore, shook his head and swore some more. It was the last straw in a week that had been filled with last straws.

"Dammit all to hell, Dad, this had better be a practical joke," he muttered.

The first straw had been Monday, when one of his subcontractors had gone belly-up. Then on Tuesday, right in the middle of Hanes Mall Boulevard at the height of rush hour traffic, one of his trucks had blown a transmission.

To add to the misery, after a solid week of rain, the entire site was a mud hole. The paving was behind schedule, the framing crew, unable to work, had celebrated by getting drunk, starting a brawl and busting up a bar. Now two of his carpenters were in jail and a third was hobbling around on crutches.

If he thought it would help, he'd get cross-eyed, rubber-lipped drunk himself, something he hadn't done since his freshman year in college. If he thought it might solve a single one of his problems, he'd go out and buy himself a carton of cigarettes and a fifth of whisky and let nature take its course.

But he didn't smoke and other than the occasional beer, he didn't drink, and besides, what good would it do to lock the barn door after the horse had bolted?

He reread the note, which was scribbled on the back of an envelope with a carpenter's pencil, judging from the smudges. It was short and to the point. "Bernice and I are honeymooning at the Blue Flamingo near Pilot Mountain. Don't forget to deposit my check on the first. Harold."

"Ah, for crying out loud, Pop," he growled. You'd think that at the age of seventy-four, a man would know better than to blow his whole damn social security check on one of these new virility drugs, start trawling the senior citizen circuit, and wind up marrying the first female he could talk into his bed.

Tucker wanted to believe he'd behaved with a little more dignity when his own marriage had ended, if working his buns off to fill in the hours until he could fall in bed exhausted could be called dignity. At least he hadn't done anything seriously stupid, much less dangerous.

"Dammit, Dad, why'd you have to go and mess up now, just when we were getting back on track?"

Tuck had been barely making it, back when his old

man announced his decision to move back home. What with the divorce settlement, child support, school fees and the building business in a temporary slump, he'd felt lucky to find an affordable dump to move into.

Shelly had got the house, along with just about everything else he owned. He'd been too numb to put up much of a fight. The anger had come later, when it was too late. By the time Harold had called to ask about coming back to North Carolina, he'd just begun to realize how empty his life was without a family to come home to.

He'd figured that having his father back home would eat up some of the loneliness that crept up on him when he was too tired to work and too restless to fall asleep.

So he'd paid for a one-way ticket and gone to meet his widowed father at the airport, expecting to see the same man he'd known all his adult life. Gray-haired, bushy-browed, wearing the familiar high-rise khakis with an open-necked dress shirt.

That wasn't what he got. Baggy shorts and a flowered shirt he could've understood. His folks had retired to Florida, after all, and the old man had stuck it out for a few years after being widowed, claiming he liked the sun and the shuffleboard, and even the occasional game of geezer softball.

The Harold Dennis who'd walked off the plane had been wearing faded jeans and a raunchy T-shirt. He'd been sporting a gray ponytail, a scraggly gray beard and one gold earring. Tucker had barely managed to turn a snort of disbelieving laughter into a greeting, but he'd hugged the old guy and told him he looked terrific. What the hell, he remembered thinking at the time—at that age, what harm could there be in kicking over the traces one last time?

Obviously, Tucker thought now, his brain hadn't been hitting on all eight cylinders. He'd be the first to admit he hadn't offered much in the way of companionship for a lonely widower, but they'd rocked along together pretty well. Once he'd settled in, Harold had looked up a few old friends, made a few new ones. On the nights when Tucker got home early enough, the two men shared a meal, watched the news on TV or a game if Tampa or the Marlins were playing. Harold was partial to Florida teams.

When the old man had taken to staying out late, Tucker hadn't thought much about it. Once baseball season was over, he'd joined a square-dancing club, started playing a little bingo. Where was the harm in that? Tuck was just glad he'd made a new life for himself after forty-six years of a good marriage. At least the rented house no longer felt so empty when Tucker came home after a twelve-hour day on the site.

The thing was—and Tucker should have thought about it sooner—the rules had changed since Harold's bachelor days. There were dangers out there a man his age couldn't even imagine. He should've warned him. Should've taken him aside for a father-son talk about scams and women and being too trusting. Reminding him to take his blood pressure medicine wasn't enough.

Instead, he'd worked right alongside his crews, buried himself in plats, blueprints and the never-ending bookwork, not to mention the constant worries over rising interest rates, rising lumber costs, tightening regulations and the shrinking market for new houses. And wondered how his son was getting along and if Shelly would allow the kid to spend at least part of the summer with his father and grandfather.

Once more Tucker read the brief note. Swearing softly, he crumpled it in his fist.

Bernice. The name didn't ring any bells. Damned if he wasn't tempted to say to hell with the whole mess. To hell with old gaffers who didn't have sense enough to keep their zipper zipped and their annuity safe. To hell with ex-wives who played dog-in-the-manger games with vulnerable kids. To hell with the feds and all the petty bureaucrats whose sole purpose was to hamstring small businessmen in red tape.

While he was at it, he tossed in a few choice words for the weather, and for whoever decreed that a man's responsibility was to work his tail off while everyone else in his family was off having fun.

Tuck's fourteen-year-old son, Jay, was away on a fly-fishing trip in Colorado with a school group. His ex-wife, Shelly, was busy squandering her settlement while she looked for another sucker. His father was wearing earrings and love beads and letting himself be reeled in by some bimbo named Bernice.

Loathing self-pity, he briefly considered straddling the old Harley and eating some dust and mosquitoes while he worked the frustration out of his system.

Trouble was, he was a worrier. Always had been. He worried about his son, who was at a vulnerable age. He worried about his partner, who was a great salesman, if little more.

And yes, dammit, he worried about the old man. Here he'd thought they were rocking along in a pretty comfortable rut, with Harold cooking breakfast and Tucker picking up pizza or barbecue on the nights when Harold wasn't going out.

Tonight, as tired as he was, Tucker had planned to stop by and pick up a six-pack, a pizza, rent a movie and indulge in an evening of quiet debauchery. Just him and the old man.

But first the truck wouldn't start, which meant he'd had to hitch a ride home, which meant no beer, no video, and no take-out supper.

And now this.

Damn.

He read the note again. Honeymooning? Shacking up was one thing, but *honeymooning?*

He swore. And then he reached for his leather jacket, stepped into his boots and swore some more.

It took a lot to ruffle Annie's composure. She prided herself on her even disposition, although lately it hadn't been as easy to maintain. But then, duty was her middle name.

Actually, it was Rebecca, but her parents used to brag on her sense of responsibility, making her all the more determined not to disappoint them. To that end she'd been valedictorian of her high school class, graduated with honors from college, which had pleased her family enormously. Personally, she'd taken more pride in never having had zits or a bad hair day, but that was something she tried not to think about, as it was both immodest and unbecoming and might even invite an attack of both.

Pride Goeth Before a Fall. She'd heard that little homily all her life. It was one of the pitfalls of being a preacher's kid. Sometimes she wondered how she might have turned out if her father had been a baker, a banker or a bartender.

Probably just as dull. James Madison Summers had been a well-respected Methodist minister. His wife, equally respected, had taken her role as a minister's wife seriously. Both of them had prided themselves on being perfect role models for the daughter who'd come along at a time in their lives when they'd given up all hope of ever having a child.

They'd been wonderful parents. Strict, but only because they loved her and wanted the best for her. An obedient child, Annie had worked hard to earn the approval of both her parents and whatever community they happened to be living in at the time, by being a credit to her upbringing.

She'd heard that one, too, more times than she cared to recall. "That Annie Summers is a credit to her folks. Might not be much to look at, but she'll be a comfort to them in their old age."

Not until years later, after both parents were gone and Annie, still unmarried with no prospects in sight, had moved into the shabby Victorian house her father had bought after he retired, did she begin to wonder if being a credit was all it was cracked up to be. Unfortunately, at this stage of her life, it had become a habit. She didn't know how to be anything else.

Cousin Bernice was her own personal plague of locusts. If ever two women were born to clash, it was Annie and Bernice Summers. It wasn't only the age difference. Annie at thirty-six was a mature, level-headed, responsible woman who wore a lot of beige, who drank one percent milk, ate whole grains, fresh fruits and vegetables and flossed every day of her life.

Bernice, at seventy-one, was a ditzy, certified flake, who dyed her hair orange, padded her bra and thought saturated fat was one of the major food groups. She wore purple-framed glasses with turquoise eye shadow, reeked of gardenia cologne and arthritis-strength linament and considered Jerry Springer the epitome of educational TV.

When Bernie's dilapidated old apartment building had been demolished to make way for a new stadium, Annie had insisted on taking her in because Bernice was a senior citizen and Annie knew her duty. Besides, they were both alone in the world except for each other, and heaven knows, there was plenty of room in the old three-story house on Mulberry.

Since then, Bernice had done everything she could think of to get Annie to set her up in another apartment, which was out of the question. It wasn't only the money, although that was a definite consideration. The truth was, Annie wasn't at all sure Cousin Bernie could look after herself, what with all the scams being perpetrated against senior citizens these days. You heard about things like that on the news all the time.

Which was another thing that drove her up the wall. Television. Annie wasn't an addict. Far from it. She turned on the set after dinner for whatever was being offered on PBS or the History Channel, or occasionally the Discovery Channel.

Bernice watched all day long. She was hooked on MTV and daytime sleaze shows. She bought herself a cheap boom box, and when she wasn't watching TV she played the thing at full volume with the bass turned all the way up—or down, as the case may be—claiming her hearing wasn't what it used to be.

Small wonder.

Lately, with the noise going full blast, she'd taken to doing something with her body she called the macaroni. Annie thought it looked as if she were counting off her body parts to be sure nothing was missing.

And she had a cat. A house cat. The Reverend and Mrs. Summers had never allowed Annie to own a pet, claiming a parsonage was no place for animals. Annie had been meaning all along to get herself a nice, quiet cat from the shelter, but that was before Bernie. Before Zen. Bernie's tomcat, Zen, was a fat, smelly, evil-tempered beast, half Persian, half coon cat, who delighted in doing his business in the indoor window boxes that lined the sun parlor and sharpening his claws on the upholstery.

Now that it was too late, Annie realized she should have laid out a few house rules right from the first, but she hadn't. Sweet, docile, dutiful Annie had been taught to respect her elders, and with all her eccentricities, Bernice was still an elder.

So she politely fumed in silence, thought bad thoughts about Zen, who obviously thought them right back at her, and wallowed in guilt over her own uncharitable nature.

But this was too much. Annie didn't know whether to believe Bernie or not. She was obviously up to something, but *marriage?*

Absurd. It was probably just another attempt to force Annie to find her an apartment and help her pay the rent. Merciful heavens, it was all Annie could do to keep up with the maintenance and repairs on her own house. She'd have sold the thing long ago except for the niggling feeling that it would be disloyal to her father, who'd been so thrilled at finally owning a house of his own, even if it was a relic in a declining neighborhood.

"Oh, Bernie, why did you have to go and do something so foolish?" she asked the cat, who stared unblinkingly from a pair of malevolent yellow eyes.

She would have to go after her, that was all there was to it. After a long day at school, dealing with the usual bureaucratic headaches, Annie had counted on leaving Bernie to her MTV and settling down in her bedroom study with a pot of tea, a little Mozart and a plate of whole-wheat crackers spread with tahini.

Being head of a family was no easy job, even when that family consisted only of a couple of cousins who had nothing in common except for a single ancestor. So far, she hadn't even found a way to explain Bernie to her fiancé and his mother.

Four and a half years ago, Annie had gotten herself engaged. Since then she'd been waiting for Eddie to work the wanderlust out of his soul, come home and find a teaching position so they could settle down and raise a real family.

Annie read the note again, ignoring the *i*s dotted

with tiny hearts. Ignoring the instructions for looking after Zen, who liked pink salmon, not dry cat food, and four percent milk, not one percent.

Somewhere upstairs a loose shutter slammed against the side of the house. Zen whipped his bushy yellow tail around her ankles and smirked at her. "No wonder you're such a fat slob," she told the creature. "I hope you get hair balls." She still hadn't forgiven him for uprooting her twelve-year-old geranium.

The Blue Flamingo was north of town on Highway 52. Miles and miles north of town. And it was raining. Annie hated driving in the rain. So did her car. Trust Bernice not to make this easy.

Prove you love me.

Is that what she was saying? Like children acting out in wildly inappropriate ways to get attention? To see if anyone cared enough to haul them back into line?

She'd read reams on the subject of behavioral problems, but as assistant principal she'd never actually been called on to deal with them in person. Mostly she dealt with the mountains of paperwork necessary to the operation of a private day school.

Almost everything Bernie did was wildly inappropriate for a woman of her age. She knew exactly how to get what she wanted, which was probably what this whole exercise was all about. It had taken her less than a day after moving in to learn how to play on Annie's overgrown sense of responsibility.

"One of these days," Annie muttered as she backed down the driveway and headed north into the teeth of a cold, blowing rain, "I'm going to do something seriously irresponsible, I swear it."

The motel was even worse than she'd expected. Totally dismal, practically deserted, it made her want to cry. If there was anything more depressing than wet concrete blocks and scraggly, dead azaleas, she didn't know what it was. Especially when seen in a drizzling rain under the flickering light of a broken neon sign.

There were six units in all. Bernie's elderly red convertible was pulled up in front of unit five. Annie took a deep breath and reminded herself once more that when children acted up, more often than not it was to gain attention. And as she hadn't been as attentive as she might have been, Annie accepted at least part of the blame.

With both her temper and her anxiety tamped down to a manageable level, she swung open the driver's side door and stepped out just as a motorcycle roared into the space beside her.

"Would you please watch where you're going?" She glared first at the rider and then down at the muddy water he'd splashed on her coattail and pantyhose.

"Lady, I'm not the one who opened a door without looking to see if it was clear."

"Well, excuse me, but the parking places are clearly marked." Annie dug out a rumpled tissue and blotted a gray-spattered shin. She knew all about men who rode motorcycles.

Well, actually, she didn't. Not personally. Her dentist, a perfectly respectable father of three, owned a Harley. He had more pictures of the machine on his office wall than he did of his children.

But there was nothing at all respectable looking about this man. He could have modeled for Bernie's favorite poster, the one showing a quartet of grungy, angry young men slouching so that their respective pelvises were thrust forward in a way that was unsettling, if not actually indecent.

Not that his was. Thrust forward, that was.

She snapped her gaze back up to his face to find that he was glaring right back at her, taking in everything from her wet shoes to her soggy silk scarf, her rain-spattered glasses, her wrinkled old trench coat and the hair that was dripping down on her face.

His opinion couldn't have been more obvious.

All right, so she was damp and a bit disheveled, at least she was decent. His jeans were not only wet, muddy and ragged, they showed every bulge on his body. And if that jaw of his had seen a razor in the past three days, she would be very much surprised. He looked like the kind of man parents of impressionable teenage girls warned their daughters against, and with just cause.

A stick figure done in shades of brown. That was Tucker's opinion of the woman who clumped past him, lifted a fist and banged on the door of number five, which, according to the zombie in what passed for an office, was registered to a Mr. and Mrs. H. Dennis.

If this was the broad who'd sunk her hooks into

his father, then the old man had lost his last marble. Coming up behind her, he said, "After you."

She glanced over her shoulder, not bothering to hide her uneasiness. "My next-door neighbor knows where I am. He's a deputy sheriff."

"Yeah, well mine's a retired dairy farmer. You going to knock again?"

"Bernice doesn't have any money. I don't know what she led you to believe, but—"

"Bernice? You're not her?"

"She. And of course I'm not."

"She, her— Lady, there's no 'of course' about it. My father's in that room with some woman named Bernice, and if you're not her—"

"She. Your *father?*"

He reached past her and pounded on the door. "Harold, open up!"

The draperies were drawn, but there were lights on inside, and the sound of TV. They waited together, Tucker and the stick figure. She was almost as tall as he was, but then, she was wearing some kind of ugly thick-soled shoes that lifted her a good two inches above the puddle of rain that had collected in front of the door.

His own boots were wet, caked with mud. So were his jeans. Riding like a bat out of hell, he'd taken back roads and shortcuts, splashing through half the mud holes in the county.

The door cracked open. One faded blue eye under a bushy gray brow peered out over the chain. "Tuck?"

"Pop, what the devil—"

"Now, don't get your shorts in a twist, Son, everything's on the up-and-up."

"The hell it—"

"Bernice, are you in there?" the stick figure called over his shoulder. She was practically draped all over him, trying to see through the crack. She smelled like wet wool and strawberries.

Strawberries?

"You must be Bernie's cousin, Annie." The eye in the doorway shifted. The door closed a moment, then opened again minus the chain. "Honey, are you decent? Looks like we've got company."

The furniture was bottom-of-the-line motel, showing both age and wear. One of Bernice's favorite TV shows was just coming on. Annie called it *World's Tackiest Videos.* On the lopsided vinyl table was an unopened bucket of fried chicken and a bottle of domestic—extremely domestic—champagne.

Dead silence persisted for all of thirty seconds, then Bernice emerged from the bathroom holding a plastic glass in each hand, and everyone started talking at once.

Harold moved to his bride's side and laid a protective arm over her shoulder. On the other side of the bed, Annie and Tucker glared at each other.

Annie got in the first shot. "I'm warning you, if your father seduced my cousin with any thought of—"

"Seduced! My father never seduced a woman in his life."

"Now, Son, you don't know—"

"And you tell your—your *cousin* for me that if she

thinks I'm going to allow some brass-haired bimbo to feather her nest at my father's expense, she can damn well think again!''

Annie gasped. "Don't you—you can't—"

"No? Try me." His eyes narrowed on a deadly glint.

"Don't tempt me," she shot back, forgetting in a single moment the training of a lifetime. "If you think for one minute some thick-necked Neanderthal with a steroid-inflated ego is going to cast aspersions at *my* cousin, you can just—"

"What did you call me?"

"If the shoe fits…" She glared at his big muddy boots.

"Now, just hush up, you two. Tucker, I taught you better than that. You've got no call to go insulting my wife.'' The older man turned to the woman at his side. "Honey, I'm ashamed to tell you, but this is my boy. He's not a bad sort, once you get to know him, I guess we just took him by surprise. Tucker, say hello to your new mama."

Annie could almost find it in her heart to feel sorry for the man called Tucker, who looked as if he'd swallowed a mouthful of fish bones. Second cousins were one thing. Father and son were another. She didn't know who was trying hardest to protect whom, but it had been battle stations from the time Tucker and Annie wedged through the doorway, both determined to rescue their respective relatives.

The older man, dressed in navy blue suit pants and a white shirt, looked as dignified as any man could look wearing an earring, a gray ponytail and matching goatee.

Bernice was at her flamboyant best in a two-piece purple silk suit and fuzzy pink bedroom slippers. There was a wilted bouquet of pink roses on the bed beside a man's coat and Bernie's best hat, the one with the rhinestones and white fake fur.

There were tears in her cousin's eyes. Oh, Lord, if they overflowed, so would the layers of turquoise shadow and navy-blue mascara. No bride, regardless of the circumstances, deserved to be seen with makeup streaking down her cheeks to settle into all the creases.

Annie's shoulders drooped as the fight went clean out of her. "You're really married, then," she said with a resigned sigh.

Bernie beamed and nodded, her clumpy lashes glistening like sweet-gum twigs in the rain. Harold's chest swelled. He looked from one to the other and his gaze returned to his son. "All right and tight. Had it done this morning. You can be the first to wish us luck."

Annie looked at Tucker, who looked back at her, daring her to speak up.

"Bernie, it's not too late," she said. "There's a new apartment going up near Clemmons. I thought we might drive out this weekend and look it over."

Bernie's lower lip trembled. She gave a little sob. Unfortunately it was the same tactic she'd tried when Annie had brought home a ten-pound sack of dry cat food instead of the salmon filet she'd requested for that damned cat.

Before things could deteriorate further, Tucker spoke up, a sickly smile on his face. "Why don't we all go out to supper somewhere and talk this over?"

The newlyweds glanced at the bucket of chicken and the bottle of champagne on the table. Bernie looked helplessly at the two glasses she'd just retrieved from the bathroom, and Tucker followed her gaze, seeing bright orange nail polish on liver-spotted hands, a gleaming gold band on the third finger, left hand.

"Okay, so maybe we could just go somewhere where there's more than two chairs and have ourselves a nice, quiet discussion."

Harold cleared his throat. "Son, I don't think you understand. This is my honeymoon. I've already made plans for the evening."

Tucker opened his mouth to argue, thought better of it and shut it again. There was nothing to be gained at this point by hurting his father's feelings and insulting the female who'd tricked him into marrying her. However, if the old bat thought for one minute that she was going to latch on to his father's social security, his annuity and his life insurance, she could damn well think again.

"Okay, so why don't we just sleep on it," he said, and groaned inwardly as he heard his own words.

Annie said, "I'll call you first thing tomorrow, Bernie."

"But not too early." Bernie looked at her bridegroom and winked, scattering a few flecks of mascara on her unnaturally rosy cheeks. "And, honey—fresh salmon, remember? Canned will do in a pinch if you can't get fresh, but remember about the milk—four percent, none of that skimmed stuff.''

Tucker didn't even try to figure that one out. He ushered the beige stick figure outside, feeling as if he'd been trapped on the twelfth floor of a ten-story building.

Without an elevator.

Two

"**A** thick-necked *Neanderthal?*" Tucker confronted Annie the minute the door closed behind them.

"Don't take it so personally, I was upset."

"With a steroid-inflated ego? What the devil is that supposed to mean?" Sure, he'd gone to college on a football scholarship, but he'd never taken steroids. "Lady, you don't know the first thing about me. How would you like it if I called you a meddling old maid with all the finesse of a front-end loader?"

She blinked owlishly behind the thick lenses. Something dark and dangerous sparked inside him. "What's the matter, don't you recognize the description? Didn't your mama teach you not to pick flaws in a man's grammar?" That still rankled.

"I didn't… Oh, shoot, I guess I did, didn't I? I'm sorry. It's probably an occupational hazard."

Her shoulders drooped. Rain had soaked through in several places. She looked so forlorn he almost relented, but dammit, a man had his pride. "Yeah, well, just don't push your luck, Annie Summers," he growled. They had finally gotten around to introductions. "My week started out in the pits and it's been downhill ever since."

"Yes, well—" He watched her throat move as she swallowed hard. "That's hardly my fault."

"You think I give a damn whose fault it is? In case it escaped your notice, that's my father—my *father* in there with that brass-haired, purple-upholstered man trap. She might think she's got it made in the shade, but take it from me, she's not going to get away with it."

"Get away with what? Taking on the care and feeding of some doddering old fool for the sheer joy of nursing him through his second childhood?" She removed her glasses, the better to glare at him. It gave her a vulnerable look, that oddly naked look of people who habitually wore glasses when seen without them.

And then the words sunk in. "His second *what?*" Muscles clenched from his jaw all the way down to his fists.

"You heard me. You can tell him for me, it won't do him a bit of good. Bernice doesn't like taking care of things. I'm the one who has to take care of her cat. She even lets plants die. As for money, all she has is her social security, and he's not going to get his hands on it."

"You think that's the reason he married her? For her money?" Tucker watched her open her mouth and then close it again as she picked her way through a minefield of possible answers. He gave her another dose. "Or maybe she's smart, like you. Is that it? She's some kind of a brain? Oh, no, I've got it. Pop was blinded by her beauty." That was hitting below the belt, but dammit, if he didn't stand up for the old man, who would?

"Bernice is—well, she's—she has a variety of interests. For one thing, she likes music, and she's really an attractive woman in her own way."

"In her own way?"

"She's, uh—colorful. Bright colors are cheerful to be around."

His gaze moved over her damp tan raincoat, her clumsy brown shoes and the few wisps of drab brown hair that straggled out from under the wet scarf tied under her chin. He didn't say a word, but when her defiant gaze fell away, he felt as if he'd just kicked the family pup off the front porch into the rain.

"Yes, well…evidently, your father sees something in her that you don't."

"Such as? Name one thing. Besides that godawful purple dress."

She rammed the glasses back on her face, but he'd caught her out. She couldn't hide behind them any longer. "You're being extremely childish," she snapped.

She had spirit, Tucker would hand her that. "Yeah, it's part of my boyish charm," he said with a nasty grin. They were both getting soaked to the skin, neither of them willing to back down an inch.

As he watched her struggle to come up with an annihilating retort, it occurred to him that between the two of them, Annie and her cousin Bernice had managed to punch a few buttons that hadn't been punched in a long time. Tucker prided himself on being a even-tempered man, both at work and in his personal life. Except for a few outbursts born of sheer frustration, he'd even managed to maintain a civilized front with Shelly. He'd done it for Jay's sake, but the truth was, picking a fight with his ex-wife had been like trying to light a wet fuse. Shelly hadn't even cared enough to fight for their marriage. The only thing she cared about was Shelly.

"Yes, well…" She had a quiet voice, but there was nothing weak about it.

"You said that before."

"You can give your father a message for me. My—that is, Bernie's lawyer will be in touch tomorrow. Tell him—tell him he'd better not try to leave town."

"Are you by any chance threatening my father?"

Long, straight nose in the air, she dived into her car, slammed the door and ground the starter a few times until the engine turned over. Torn between frustrated anger and reluctant admiration, he watched as she scratched out of the parking lot and headed south.

"Lawyer, my sweet ass," he growled as he caught up with her and roared past, a few minutes later. He'd been taken to the cleaners by the flock of buzzards Shelly had hired to pick his bones. Damned if he was going to stand by and see the same thing happen to his father.

Annie pressed the heels of her hands against her aching eyes the next morning and wondered what the downside of retiring at age thirty-six would be, aside from a severe lack of funds. Terminal boredom, probably. After spending hours last night alternately worrying about personnel problems at school and worrying about Bernice, she'd fallen asleep just as the sky was turning gray and woken up with one of those headaches that was impervious to feverfew and even acetominophen.

Yesterday had been endless. Three teachers on maternity leave, an outbreak of head lice, plus the latest mandate to come down from Washington, to be translated from bureaucratese into something even her boss, with his limited vocabulary, could understand. And of course, there had been Bernie's surprise elopement yesterday.

Annie had promised herself she'd try again to get in touch with Eddie and see if they couldn't meet somewhere. Asia. Africa. The moon. As engagements went, hers was extremely unsatisfactory. Sometimes she wondered why she even bothered to hang on to the pretense.

In the beginning she'd done it because it was all she had, or was ever likely to have, but that was before Bernice. Before she'd spent one more in a long line of restless nights, trying to peel back the layers of Annie Summers in case there was something underneath it all—heaven only knew what—that would explain why a lifetime of doing the right thing had brought her to a point where she couldn't think of a single good reason for continuing to do it.

Except for the year she'd broken her leg in two places and the year she'd come down with a bad case of food poisoning, she'd earned perfect attendance records at school and Sunday School, simply because it was expected of her.

Outstanding grades? She'd worked hard to earn them because it was expected of her. Graduated with honors from an all-girl college for the same reason. Camp counselor, scout leader—she'd done the whole bit.

"It's up to you to give back to your community, because of who you are," her father had drilled into her from the age of pigtails, pinafores and piano lessons. Dutifully, she had obeyed, without ever wondering until it was too late just who Annie Summers was supposed to be. She'd done, and she'd been, and she'd given the very best she could do and give and be, sacrificing—

Well, not sacrificing a whole lot, if you didn't count not being able to stay out late or date the boy she'd been dying to date in high school. Not that he'd ever asked her, but he might have if she'd had the courage to give the right signals.

As if she'd even know how to send a signal. At the age of thirty-six, she was engaged to a political activist who was determined to go out and save the world from hunger and decadent capitalism before he came home and settled down to carve out his own slice of the pie. She hadn't heard from him in almost six months. But then, Eddie had never been a very good correspondent.

Some love life. So where did she get off, trying to manage Bernie's love affair? Telling her she shouldn't run off and marry a man because he might try to take advantage of her? Maybe they were taking advantage of each other. Taking advantage of whatever time they had left for whatever mutual pleasure it provided. If she was still waiting for Eddie by the time she was Bernie's age, she might even start looking around for a lonely widower herself.

"Get off my feet, you noisy old tomcat." She kicked aside the covers, dislodging the cat who had taken up residence on the foot of her bed sometime during the night, purring his fool head off and scratching his various itches.

Bleary-eyed, she made it to the kitchen to put on the kettle for tea. Glancing outside, she saw that the rain had stopped, but the clouds still hung dark and heavy and sullen. "Story of my life," she muttered to the cat, who had decided to wrap his tail around her ankles to see if he couldn't trip her into falling headfirst into the refrigerator. Unthinkingly she reached down and scratched him behind his ears.

By focusing on the morning paper while she ate her standard breakfast of fruit, tea and whole-grain cereal, she almost managed to avoid thinking about her immediate problems. To put things into perspective, there was always Washington, China and the Middle East.

The phone waited until she was halfway through

brushing her teeth to ring. She caught it on the forth ring and gargled, "Hewwo?"

"Annie? This is Bernice, are you all right?"

"Of course I'm all right, if you don't count having to swallow a mouthful of toothpaste. Where are you? What happened? Do you need me to come get you?" Bernice's old junker was inclined to be temperamental.

"Why would I need you to do that?"

"Well, I don't know, I only thought— Bernie, it's barely eight o'clock in the morning, what's going on?"

"Well, now that you mention it, you could do me a favor if you've got time. You said you were going to call, didn't you?"

Annie patted her bare foot and waited. Bernie's demands were never straightforward. "It's Saturday. I've got time. If you want to try and get the whole mess annulled, I'll meet you wherever you say, and I promise not to ask any questions, all right?"

"I don't want to get anything annulled. Besides, it's too late for that. And believe me, Harold doesn't need any of that Vigaro stuff, either."

"Any *what?*"

"You know. It's been all over the news since last year."

"Bernie, what on earth—no, don't tell me, I don't even want to know."

"Oh, for pity's sake, I knew you'd be like this, you always are."

"Like what?" Annie wailed, gesturing wildly with

her toothbrush. "I'm not being like anything, just tell me what you called about, please!"

"You're just waiting for a chance to say you told me so, aren't you? You're just like your father always was, you know that?"

It was on the tip of her tongue to deny it, but this was not the time. "Bernie, what are you calling about?" she asked with as much patience as she could muster. "Like Daddy? I'm nothing at all like Daddy. Daddy was the sweetest, kindest man alive."

"Maybe, but he could be a real pain in the rear end."

"So can I. What's your point, Bernie?"

"It's about Harold's boy."

"Harold's what?"

"You met him yesterday. Tucker. He was here the same time you were, don't you remember?"

"I remember," Annie snapped. She remembered all too well. The memory had a lot to do with why she'd spent so many fruitless hours peeling back the layers of Annie Summers, trying to find out if there was anything worth salvaging under all those years of conditioning.

"Yes, well, Harold's been trying to call him, but he doesn't answer his phone, and—"

"You want me to go see if he's all right? Bernie, have you lost your mind?"

"Oh, he's probably all right—I mean, why wouldn't he be? But the thing is, Harold forgot his blood pressure medicine, and he can't remember Tucker's mobile number, and it's not listed, so since you don't have to go to school, would you mind driving out to where he's working and asking him to bring it out to the motel? Harold says it's probably on the kitchen windowsill.''

Annie rolled her eyes. From the sun parlor came the sound of dirt being scratched onto the tile floor. "Why can't Harold go get his own medicine?" Her jaw was tightening up again. Tension always did it to her.

"Well, because he can't, that's all. Do that for me, Annie, and I'll never ask you for anything again, I promise."

"What about your cat?"

"I'll take him off your hands just as soon as Harold and I find a place to live."

Annie wasn't at all sure she wanted to get rid of her cousin, or even her cousin's cat. Somebody in the Summers family had to take responsibility for the flakier members, and she was obviously elected. Eddie would just have to understand.

Which was how she came to be splashing through a muddy construction site, dodging ruts and panel trucks, and knocking on the door of a brown metal trailer some forty-five minutes later. Somewhat to her surprise, the sign on the door said Dennis Construction. Which Dennis? Father? Son? Both?

Not that it mattered.

When the door was flung open, she nearly tumbled down the mud-slick step. "Oh, for God's sake, *now* what?" Tucker Dennis exclaimed plaintively.

"Don't take your nasty temper out on me, I'm only here to do your father a favor."

"Yeah, sure you are. If you can pry your cousin's

hooks out of his hip pocket, that'll be favor enough to suit me.''

''Fine. I'll tell your father's wife you refuse to take him his blood pressure medicine. Do you know the name of his physician, just in case?''

''What blood pressure medicine?'' He opened the door wider and muttered, ''You might as well come inside.''

Annie did, but only because she wasn't sure he wouldn't grab her by the arm and yank her inside if she refused. He had that look about him.

The interior was no more inviting than the exterior. A stack of boxes in one corner. A dull green file cabinet, a gray metal desk, a scarred draftsman's table and two tan metal chairs. If you didn't count the red mud that had been tracked inside, the only bit of color to be found was in the row of hard hats that hung over a small rusty refrigerator—two white, a blue, an orange and a yellow—and a feed store calendar on the opposite wall.

''You might as well sit down.'' He waved her to one of the two worn oak chairs. ''I've got a few things to say to you.''

''The medicine.''

''In a minute.''

She took a deep breath and tried to remember the lessons of a lifetime, but nothing in all the years she'd spent among decent, civilized people had prepared her for dealing with a surly, motorcycle-riding construction worker in an ugly metal trailer out in the muddy middle of nowhere.

So she sat. Back straight, ankles crossed and hands

resting one of top of the other on her lap. But no amount of outward composure could prevent the color from rising to stain her cheeks.

Tucker flexed his fingers, stiff from hours of clutching a pencil and years of working with his hands. Incipient arthritis. Wet weather didn't help. He studied the woman seated across the desk from him, reluctantly revising his earlier opinion. She wasn't as old as he'd thought yesterday, nor quite as plain. But her raincoat was every bit as ugly as he remembered it and so were her shoes. Nor had her disposition undergone any miraculous overnight transformation.

"So what is it you want me to do?"

"Go home and get your father's medicine and take it to him. I suppose."

"You suppose?"

"That's the message I was given. You didn't answer your home phone, and your father couldn't remember your mobile, so Bernie called me to pass on the message."

"Harold knows how to reach me here."

She shrugged. "All I know is what I was told. If you're too busy to be bothered, then I'll call Bernie and tell her—"

"Oh, for Pete's sake, just hang on a minute will you?"

Annie hung on. Just barely. She was cold. Her head still ached, and there was something about the man that set her teeth on edge. As a rule, she reacted to people on an intellectual level. There was nothing faintly intellectual about her reaction to Tucker Dennis. She felt like grabbing him with both hands and shaking him!

"I can turn up the heat if you're cold."

"Thanks, but I won't be here long enough."

He shrugged. "Your call. I thought I saw you shiver."

Outside, the rain began to drum down on the metal, making it impossible to carry on a normal conversation. Annie winced as her headache reacted to the noise.

Raising his voice over the roar, Tucker yelled, "Okay, I'll go as soon as the rain slacks off."

"What?" She took off her glasses and pressed the heels of her hand into her eyes, and he was struck all over again by how vulnerable she looked without them.

Yeah, sure she was. Vulnerable like a baby copperhead, which was about twice as lethal as an adult specimen.

"I said—" Instead of repeating himself, he stood, moved around behind her and nudged the controls of the gas heater. She wasn't wearing her scarf today. With her head lowered, about four inches of bare neck showed between her collar and the wad of damp brown hair knotted at the back of her head. Her skin looked as if it had never seen the sun.

"Headache?" he asked, his voice sounding gruff even to his own ears.

The impression of vulnerability disappeared along with the sliver of bare nape as she raised her head and squared her shoulders. Tucker thought of the way his father used to massage his mother's shoulders when she had one of her tension headaches. He wondered who massaged away this woman's pain. Or if anyone did.

And then he wondered why the hell he was wondering.

By the time Annie drove off a few minutes later, the rain had let up. Even so, the going was treacherous. She slithered twice on the mud-slick road, telling herself she'd done all she could do. If Harold's blood pressure shot sky-high, it was his son's fault, not hers. She could hardly break into his house and get the stuff herself. Didn't even know where he lived.

All the same, she was relieved when she slowed down to turn onto Highway 52 to see one of the trucks with the Dennis Construction logo on the door pull away from the construction site. Evidently the man possessed some vestigial sense of responsibility.

Ruffian was the term that came to mind. That had been one of her father's favorite descriptions. He'd attached it to hardened criminals, aggressive drivers and the kids who trampeled the parsonage flowerbeds. She hadn't heard anyone use it in years.

"Oh, God, Annie, you're a walking anachronism," she muttered.

The school secretary, all of twenty-two years old, would have said—*had* said, in fact on more than one occasion—"Get a life, Annie."

Good advice. Annie had done her best, only her best didn't seem to be good enough.

Three

The marriage was perfectly legal. The bride and groom were both of age and of sound mind, although there was some slight doubt about that last part, at least to Annie's way of thinking.

Tucker's, too. He left her in no doubt of his opinion when he showed up to collect Bernie's spare reading glasses a day or so later.

"About time you got home," he growled. He'd been waiting when she'd driven up, tired, hungry and burdened with a stack of books, two sacks of groceries and the dry cleaning she'd picked up on the way home.

She shot him a look that said it all. Her headache might be gone, but as usual the last day of the term had been utter chaos. And now, with Bernie's situation, any hope of getting away for a few days was gone. "If your father thinks he's landed in a bed of roses, he just might be in for a surprise. Bernie's not the easiest person to live with."

"That I can believe." He looked as if he wanted to say more, but thought better of it. Instead, he took the dry cleaning from her, followed her inside and looked around for a place to deposit it. She indicated the coat tree that stood between the glass-paneled door and the entrance into the front parlor, never mind that no one had parlors these days. Her house did. Two of them, front and sun. One had leaky windows, the other a cracked ceiling.

Her toe struck one of Zen's toys, a pair of small brass balls linked together by a dangling tab, and she kicked it aside, too tired even to pick it up and toss it into his basket. She liked animals, truly she did, but this particular creature took a diabolical delight in irritating her. "All right, what is it this time? Your father forgot his corn plasters?" she asked, resigned to having to wait a few more minutes before she could change into her robe and slippers, brew herself a cup of strawberry tea and zone out, as the schoolkids put it. Whatever it meant, it sounded like just what she needed. Nirvana.

"Your cousin needs her glasses."

"The last time I saw her she was wearing her glasses." Annie removed her own and closed her eyes momentarily. It didn't help. When she opened them again, he was still there.

"I only know what she said."

"Do you suppose she means her reading glasses?

She never wears those in mixed company." Drugstore magnifying glasses, they were stronger than her purple-framed bifocals. The only time she wore them was when she was studying the *TV Guide* so she could highlight her weekly selections with Annie's yellow marker.

"So call her and tell her that. She's been trying to reach you all day."

"She knows very well how to reach me. This is the last day of the school term. I was there all day. She could've called the office and left word."

He shrugged. The man had shoulders like a road scraper. "You're a teacher?"

"Assistant principal." He knew that. He was just trying to irritate her. Refusing to be irritated, she stood there, books in one arm, two sacks of groceries in the other, while he looked her up and down. Whatever he was thinking, he had better sense than to say anything, but it was painfully clear that his opinion was not particularly flattering.

"Oh, all right. Wait here and I'll see if I can find them." She dumped the books on the hall table and stalked off toward the kitchen, where she deposited the two sacks of produce. Apples and collard greens, probably the last of the season. Feeling like a criminal, she'd broken open the bundled leaves in the store and selected only the young, tender ones, telling herself it was no different from selecting unblemished apples, and anyone with a grain of sense did that.

He was right behind her. "Would you mind hurrying? This is my son's night to call, and it'll take me an hour at least to run out to the motel."

Tough turnips, Annie wanted to say, but didn't. She could think of several things she'd like to say, but didn't. Instead, she rummaged in all the places a pair of reading glasses might be lurking. Bernie wasn't known for her orderliness, nor her predictability.

"Would you mind looking in the drawer in the hall table?" It was the last place they'd be, but she needed some breathing room. Men like Tucker Dennis took up more than their fair share of space.

His son? He was married?

Not that it mattered one way or another. All the same, she was somewhat surprised. He hadn't struck her as a domestic animal when he'd roared up on that monster bike of his, scowling from here to Sunday, with a week's growth of whiskers meant to impart an I-can't-be-bothered-to-shave attitude.

Since then, he'd shaved. Come to think of it, his jaw had been only lightly shadowed the day she'd driven out to his construction site to pass on the message about the blood pressure medicine. He might not be a genuine, dyed-in-the-wool ruffian, but he was obviously the next best thing. Or the next worst.

"I don't suppose..."

Her heart flopped over and she spun around, slapping a hand over her chest. "I didn't hear you."

"Sorry. Wet boot soles don't make much noise." He held up a pair of gold-framed specs that had been right there in the same drawer when she'd moved into the house. Uncertain what to do with them—tossing them in the trash seemed heartless, as her father had considered them worth keeping—she'd left them where she'd found them.

"No, those aren't the ones. Bernie's are round, with dark brown plastic frames and a pink pearl hanger."

"A pink pearl what?" He reached over and righted the plastic sack of apples just as it started to tumble.

"You know—one of those stringy things that hang around the neck so you don't lose your glasses."

"So how come they're lost?"

Amazing. The man actually smiled. It was fleeting, but nice while it lasted. "If you'll wait a minute, I'll run upstairs and look in her room."

"I'll put away your apples. These plastic bags aren't very stable."

She was tempted to say, "Whatever," a response that was heard a lot around school, and not just from the students. As in she would do whatever it took to get out of this mess. Whatever it took to get him out of her house.

But she didn't. Annie simply wasn't a "whatever" kind of woman.

"I found them," she called out from halfway down the stairs a few minutes later. "And would you mind taking Bernie her mail, as long as you're going out there anyway?"

Tucker had dumped the fruit into the bowl on the table, helping himself to one of her apples. He was studying the snapshot of Eddie holding a naked brown baby and squinting into the sunlight. She'd stuck it on the refrigerator in a magnetic frame as a constant reminder of a man she found all too easy to forget.

He took the mail, glanced at it absently, and said,

"AARP, Special Olympics and an *International Male* catalog. Do I need to get her to sign for it?"

"Yes, why don't you do that?" Her eyes took on a steely glint, and Tucker told himself he deserved it. His company manners had deteriorated since his divorce.

"Sorry. Any messages?" He shoved the mail into his hip pocket and waited for her to have the last word. He knew her type. She'd manage to have it, anyway.

"Just one. You can ask your father how long he plans to keep my cousin in that disreputable place."

"Why? Has she been complaining? Funny, she looked pretty comfortable last time I saw her."

"Bernie's never been one to complain." He lifted an eyebrow at that. "That doesn't mean your father didn't get her there under false pretenses."

"You think he ensorcelled her?"

"He en-*what?*"

"It means—"

"I know what it means!"

"Yeah, well—I read it in one of my son's comic books."

"Why am I not surprised?"

"Hey, don't knock comic books. You'd be amazed at what you can learn from those things."

She rolled her eyes, and even behind the lenses, he couldn't help but notice their size, clarity and color. He wondered if she ever wore contacts and decided she wasn't the type. That would suggest vanity. Whatever her faults, vanity probably wasn't one of them. About all she had to be vain about, so far as he could see, was a pair of world-class ankles, and she ruined the effect of those by wearing ugly platform shoes.

She held out the glasses, and he took them and started to ram them into his pocket along with the mail, then thought better of it. "I don't suppose you have a case for these things?"

"No, I don't."

"No problem. I'll just toss 'em in the toolbox. They'll be safe enough," he said, straight-faced.

"Oh, for heaven's sake, I'll find you something, all right?"

"Forget it, I'll just hang 'em from my rearview mirror by that little thingamajiggy, that suit you?"

As frowns went, hers was a beaut. Sour, dried-up old maid, no wonder her cousin had bolted. She must've been hell on wheels to live with. Whatever else he was, Harold was no grouch.

She gave him a hand towel to wrap them in, then practically shoved him out the front door. Tucker thought, *Lady, you're no more eager to get rid of me than I am to see the last of you!*

But then she went and spoiled it. "Well…thank you for coming by for Bernie's glasses. And for taking them to her. Oh, and if you find out anything, I would appreciate being kept informed."

I would appreciate being kept informed. I'll just bet you would, Miss Prissy-pants. "Like what?"

"Well, you know. Where they mean to live? That sort of thing? I don't suppose even your father plans to stay on in that flamingo place permanently."

"I wouldn't count on that. Pop used to have pretty good judgment, but these past few days make me wonder...." When she bristled, all ready to launch, he said hastily, "Okay, I'll find out what I can, but Harold can be pretty stubborn when you get his back up. Busting in on his honeymoon wasn't exactly the most tactful thing we could've done."

"Well, don't look at me. All I was trying to do is rescue my cousin before it was too late."

"Same here. It would've helped if I'd had a little advance warning. He mentioned somebody named Bernie a few times, but I figured it was one of his card-playing buddies."

Annie wasn't about to admit that she'd long since grown tired of Bernie's constant complaints and tuned her out for the most part. Sighing, she watched him stride off down her front walk, past the crack where the oak roots were buckling the concrete, through the front gate that was her pride and joy, being the only intact wrought iron one on the block.

She was still standing in the front door, letting in the cold damp air, when she realized she was staring at his backside, admiring the way he walked, shoulders swaying over a narrow, muscular rear end. Slamming the heavy door hard enough to rattle the beveled glass panels, she muttered, "Oh, for heaven's sake, woman, get a grip."

Tucker didn't know what to do. On the one hand he felt partly responsible for the mess his father was in, because he'd been too preoccupied lately to notice what was going on. He'd read enough statistics to know there were a lot more single women than there were available men, and once a man became single again he was considered fair game.

Hell, he was probably fair game himself, only he avoided places where he might become a target. Harold had invited him to a few dances, but he'd been either too busy or too tired to go.

Come to think of it, his father had seemed relieved. Maybe he hadn't really wanted a son tagging along to cramp his style. Maybe the old man was just being polite. Or feeling sorry for him.

Tucker turned that idea over in his mind a time or two and examined it. Since when was a man who chose of his own free will to stay single considered an object of pity?

Not that he'd been the one to choose. The divorce had been Shelly's idea, and rather than subject Jay to any more of the silent battleground their marriage had become, he'd gone along with it. Let her walk all over him. Let her take everything—the car, the house with his newly outfitted office over the double garage—everything except for the one thing that mattered most.

He'd insisted on his rights where Jay was concerned, but Shelly had been named custodial parent. At that point Tucker hadn't even had a home, much less one suitable for a child. It had been Shelly who had found a school in Connecticut that worked with kids whose lives had been messed up by their parents' mistakes. Once Tucker had been convinced that it was a good idea, for now, at least, he'd forked over whatever it took, which was considerable, and then settled in to deal with his own guilt for being a party to the divorce that had screwed up his son's life.

In the long run, he figured, a man was safer without a woman. He might miss the regular sex, but then sex with Shelly had never been all that regular. Once the honeymoon ended, she'd quickly lost interest. He might miss the companionship, but Shelly's idea of companionship was dressing up in fancy clothes for some boring society shindig with a bunch of equally boring stiffs. Once he'd invited her to go to a baseball game with him and Jay, and she'd looked at him as if he'd lost his mind.

It was late. He was tired. The weather was depressing as hell. He thought about lighting a fire and decided it was too much trouble. Besides, first he'd have to haul out the ashes and bring in some wood. So he sat there in front of the small, cold fireplace in the cheerless, white-painted living room and read the paper, or as much of it as he was interested in, dropped it beside his chair, leaned his head back and closed his eyes. He hadn't really done enough physical work today to be this tired. Maybe he needed vitamins or something. He'd eaten one of Annie's apples. That was a good start. An Annie a day keeps the the doctor awa-a-ay....

Evidently he dozed off, because when the phone rang it took him a minute to pull himself together. It was the sound of his son's voice that made him aware for one unguarded moment of how deep loneliness could run, once a man let it get a foothold.

"How's it been going, son? You back at school yet? How was the fly-fishing trip?"

He listened, making the appropriate comments and trying to picture every catch, every campfire, every practical joke—wishing he could have been a part of it all.

"Dad, I need some new waders. My feet grew another whole size."

"Well, okay—I guess we can manage that. What about shoes?"

"No prob. I traded with this guy that's bigger than me. Three CDs for a pair of good hikers that are practically new."

"Tell your mother to pick out whatever you need, I'll take care of it."

"Mom's going to Naples. She said she'd call, but she hasn't yet."

"Naples, Italy or Naples, Florida?"

"There's a Naples in Italy, too?"

"Last I heard there was."

"Yeah, well, I guess she's just going to the one in Florida with some friends. This guy's got a place there, and she said it was real cool, with a swimming pool and all. Hey, I aced my math test, did I tell you?"

Jay's problem had never been math. Tucker didn't ask about his other classes. He'd know soon enough.

They talked some more about fishing, and about a fly rod with a broken tip that needed repairing. From past experience, Tucker suspected it would cost almost as much to fix the old one as it would to replace it. He decided to spring for a new rod and save the old one so that Jay could learn how to repair his own gear.

Then Jay asked about his grandfather. Tucker briefly debated telling him about Harold's latest adventure. In the end he didn't mention it. No point in worrying the boy prematurely, when the whole affair would probably blow over by the time Jay got home for spring break.

It had damned well better. If Harold was counting on moving into his old room with a woman, then they were going to have to do some renegotiating. Five rooms with no frills and damned little privacy might do for a couple of men and a part-time kid, but a woman—that was another thing altogether. No way was he going to let that female move into his house.

The site was begining to dry out. The roofers figured they could get back on the job by tomorrow, barring more rain, and the framers were already at it. Glory hallelujah, as his mama used to say.

Tucker sat astride the Harley and gazed with satisfaction on the tract of land his partner had christened Half Moon Lake, for the curved six-acre pond that had until a few years ago been used to water livestock. Dean Barger, his partner, had bought the property at auction, and immediately started looking around for a construction firm to help him develop it.

Tucker, still raw from his divorce and needing a project to dive into, had taken him up on his offer. Dean had wanted starter houses, cheaply built, on the smallest lots possible under the county's building codes.

It had been Tucker who'd held out for six-to seven-acre plots, with one show house and the rest to be built to order according to the covenant they'd drawn up. So far, things were moving better than expected. The show house had been snapped up the first week, and several more sites had been sold since, with new houses already under construction. They were trying to open up the back section now, with Dean handling sales and Tucker overseeing grading, paving and health permits.

Those parcels would sell, just like the others. Tucker almost hated to see it happen. He'd spent a lot of time roaming those woods, looking down on the pond, trying to site each house so the biggest and best trees could be spared.

Hearing the sound of a vehicle turning off the highway, he dismounted and headed for his office. This was no time for the damned perk tester to be showing up, after all the rain they'd had lately. The man swore methods had improved, and that soil saturation no longer mattered. But he'd heard tales from his father about the old days when, before permitting a septic tank, someone from the health department would pick a spot, dig a hole, pour in a bucket of water and then wait to see how long it took to soak in.

"Mr. Dennis! Wait a minute, will you?"

Oh, hell, it was the Summers woman. He turned and waited until she reached the bottom of the hill, wondering if she was going to be dumb enough to pull into the clearing between the Dumpster and the Port-o-let. Wondering if he ought to warn her. It might not look it, but it was slick as boiled okra, which was why none of the workers parked there. He had to admit there were a few places on the property that didn't perk. That happened to be one of them.

So he warned her. It wasn't that he was a good guy, it was purely self-interest. If she got stuck, he'd be the one to have to pull her out. He waved her to the spot beside the plumber's van, and she parked there and got out, minus the tan raincoat and the scarf. It was the first time he'd seen her without the coat, and he was surprised to discover that in brown tweed slacks and a fuzzy turtleneck sweater, she wasn't quite the stick figure he'd thought.

Her hair was tied back with a scarf instead of rolled up into a knot at the back of her head. It made a difference.

Not that he was interested one way or another. Still, it just went to show that a man couldn't judge by first impressions alone. Or even second and third ones.

She sounded breathless, as if she'd run all the way. There were patches of color in her cheeks. Actually she wasn't at all bad looking, if you liked the type. Long, oval face, long straight nose, large gray eyes and a full, expressive mouth. She had the kind of understated looks that could grow on a man if he wasn't careful.

Yeah, like warts.

"Got a problem?" he asked.

"I'm afraid so. It's your father's driver's license. Actually, it's more than that. I think we need to talk."

The sun was out, but there was a brisk northwest wind. The temperature was barely out of the forties. Tucker sighed. Sighing wasn't something he did a whole lot of, although lately...

"Okay, you might as well come on inside."

Four

Annie took a folding chair without waiting to be asked. This was getting to be something of a habit. "You know of course that they took Bernie's car instead of your father's."

"Harold doesn't own a car. He drives one of the company trucks when he drives at all. Usually one of his friends picks him up."

"Yes, well, Bernie has arthritis in the top of her feet."

"The top of her feet? I never heard of that."

She shrugged. "It bothers her now and then, usually in wet weather or when she goes from flats to high heels. It's worse in her right foot. Anyway, she says she'd just as soon not drive, so would you mind looking in the top dresser drawer, left-hand side, in your father's room and bringing his driver's license out to the motel?''

Tucker uttered a four letter word, then apologized. ''Yeah, sure. I guess. Did she happen to say when they're coming home?''

''Whose home, yours or mine?''

''God only knows. And here I was, dreading the time when Jay was old enough to get into trouble. He's nearly fourteen, and so far we haven't had any serious problems.''

Annie just nodded. Working with school age children, she knew all about the crazy stunts they could pull. ''I told them you'd be out this afternoon. I'm afraid I promised Bernie you'd pick up a bucket of chicken on your way. Just as sort of a—you know, a goodwill offering?''

''Where's all this goodwill supposed to come from?'' He sounded irritable. He looked harried. Annie could almost find it in her heart to feel sorry for the man. Bernice was only her second cousin, but Harold was Tucker's father. It had to cause concern.

''I'll pay for it,'' she offered, ''since you're delivering.''

They went back and forth on that subject a few times, with Annie trying tactfully to discover just how solvent Bernie's new husband was. If he'd been planning to live on his bride's tiny income, he was out of luck. SOL, as the students put it. It meant something like sure out of luck.

Harold lifted his bride's foot onto his lap and began massaging liniment into the affected area. His knees bothered him now and again. His feet never had. They'd both sat out a few square dances, which was how they'd happened to renew their acquaintance several months ago.

"Remember that time you and Hoss Stoggins got hung up halfway down Pilot Mountain and had to be rescued?"

"Don't remind me." He chuckled and stroked the delicate bones. "How'd you hear about it, anyway? I hardly even knew you then."

"You were famous. All the girls were crazy about you. If you hadn't been engaged to Martha, I'd have gone after you myself." She waited a minute, leaning back on the stack of pillows, her eyes closed. "You miss her, don't you?"

"Who, Martha? Yes ma'am, I reckon I do. Man can't spend more than half his life with a woman and not miss her when she goes. That doesn't mean I don't think the world of you, but—"

"Oh, I know that. It's different, though, at our age. I missed out on a whole lot, what with looking after Mama and not being pretty and all, but I never let it get me down."

"Now, Bernie, you're a fine-looking woman." His fingers strayed up her shin, over the fine blue veins. The room smelled of liniment, Old Spice, Obsession and Pine Sol.

"We both know I was never in Martha's class, but she's gone, Lord bless her, and I'm still here. If I was in her place, I'd want to know you were being looked after."

"I know. That's what worries me about that boy."

"Annie, too, poor girl. I tried to set a good example, but it didn't do a speck of good. Claims she's engaged, but she doesn't wear a ring. Keeps a picture on the refrigerator. Me, I think she cut it out of National Geographic. She never talks about him. I declare, watching a girl wither on the vine without ever getting ripe, it's a pure shame, is what it is. Remember what we were talking about day before yesterday? About him and her, I mean. You reckon it might work?"

Harold shook his head. "Hard to tell. Tuck's been scared off women. He's even forgot how to have a good time."

"Annie never learned how." She ran her fingernail over the seam at the side of his khakis. His ponytail was gone. He'd let Bernie trim his hair while they'd watched *Jeopardy* last night. Proving he still had a few good swinging years left in him no longer seemed so important. She liked his earring, though. He'd kept it, even with short hair.

"I wish we could think of some way to get 'em to come out here together," Harold mused. "Maybe seeing a pair of newlyweds up close and personal, like they say on the TV, might give 'em an idea. Might not, though. Tuck didn't take to marriage. Some men don't, I reckon."

"Some women don't ever get the chance. Me, I never gave up. Look on the bright side, I always say." Bernie smiled a cat-and-canary smile. "I told Annie if we weren't here, to leave the license in the office. Poor girl, she hates to be out alone after dark. Just like her mama. No gumption at all."

"Reckon she'll get Tuck to drive her out here?"

"Wouldn't be surprised. It's a right long drive," Bernie said smugly, patting the angel pin on her lapel. "Want to drive into town? We could do a few turns around the mall, my foot's not that bad off."

"Maybe pick up a couple of corn dogs and bring 'em back? There's some pretty good TV tonight."

"I wish we had a freezer in here. Ice cream goes real nice with television. Mmm, right there." Bernie closed her eyes as Harold's strong fingers manipulated her metatarsals. "You've got good feeling hands, Mr. Dennis."

"Yours aren't half bad, Mrs. D," he retorted, and they both started to smile.

Tucker bought chicken. A bucketful. As he flat out refused to allow Annie to pay for the chicken, much less fill up his gas tank, she insisted on riding with him. "I feel guilty making you drive all the way out there again. I know you're busy, and besides, it must feel odd, visiting your father on his honeymoon."

He didn't want to talk about it. Truth was, he was still unsettled from the way his body had reacted when he'd helped her into his truck. With those shoes of hers, she could have made it easy, even in the four-by-four, but he'd acted without thinking, and now he couldn't *stop* thinking.

Thinking about the way she was built. Lean, but flexible. The kind of woman built to weather a storm without breaking. Thinking about how she stood up for that dingbat cousin of hers when it was obvious that the woman drove her up a wall.

Steadfast was a word that came to mind. Trouble was, it wasn't the only word that came to mind. With his hands on her waist as he'd helped her into the truck, his reaction had been pure-D male.

It just went to show he was in worse shape than he'd thought, if touching a woman through a few layers of wool—a woman who had all the sex appeal of a bowl of cold oatmeal—could turn him on.

Sex and food. The necessities of life. A man could go only so long without either and stay sane and healthy.

"How long is this honeymoon supposed to last?" Annie asked when they'd driven several miles in silence.

Tucker took a deep breath, inhaling a mixture of fried chicken, wet woolens and soap. Not even the scented kind, just plain soap, the kind his mama used to call castile. "Beats me," he said. "Until the money runs out, I guess. Got any clue when that'll be?"

"Not really. Bernie doesn't discuss her finances. I think she has a tiny pension, but it can't be much. She worked for thirty-six years as a clerk in a department store, and the store went out of business several years ago."

"Harold invested in mutual funds when I bought out his share of the business. I doubt if he's dug into them, but I'm not about to ask."

Annie sighed and refolded her hands in her lap. They were still skirting around the issue of the newlyweds' solvency, but at least they were no longer openly hostile. Perhaps they could work things out after all.

"I do know there was some sort of function at the Golden Oldies Club earlier this month. Bernie had her eye on a certain dress, hoping it would go on sale, but it never did. I offered to make her something to wear, but I only do plain sewing, and she insisted on georgette."

"Who's Georgette?"

"It's this real thin—well, it's sort of like—"

"Never mind."

"I hate it when anyone says *never mind* or *whatever*. They might as well tell you they're not interested in anything you have to say."

Tucker turned off the highway and followed the two-lane to the motel parking lot. It was empty except for a '79 Eldorado parked outside the office. They weren't here. "You're right. I'm sorry. Look, they're not here. We can wait a few minutes if you want to. So go ahead and tell me about this George guy. He sells dresses, and Bernice couldn't afford to buy one from him, which means she's not exactly rolling in it. Why am I not surprised?"

She looked at him as if he'd suddenly started spouting a foreign language. One thing Tucker had learned in their brief association was that for an uptight female who wore ugly shoes, ugly clothes, ugly glasses and reeked of unscented soap, Ms. Summers had a way of expressing herself that could be downright lethal. For one thing, her vocabulary was better than his. He'd studied engineering, not English lit.

Shelly used to rub his nose in it, calling him an uncouth redneck who never got past being a football star in high school.

Hell, he didn't even watch football anymore. Didn't have time. But when a guy got shoved, the natural thing was to shove back.

She was watching him from the corner of her eye as if she could read his mind. So what if she could, he hadn't been thinking anything that wasn't the gospel truth. The woman wore ugly clothes because she didn't want to attract masculine attention?

Okay by him. He wasn't exactly in the market for an affair, even if he had time for it. His life was complicated enough without that. All the same, maybe he should suggest she start wearing boots to cover those sexy ankles of her. And tie that rag over her head again to cover her hair. You wouldn't think straight, brown hair would be so interesting, but hers was. In an understated sort of way.

"I'm worried about them," Annie murmured. He'd noticed her voice, too. It was quiet, what you might call well modulated. Shelly's was sort of shrill, but then, Shelly was usually whining, nagging or chewing him out. Annie might bitch, but she did it in a well-bred way.

"You think I'm not?" They watched the highway as they sat there listening to the sound of cooling metal.

"Of course you are. Your father's blood pressure, after all. But as I said before, Bernie's arthritis bothers her most on days like this. Not that she'll admit it."

"Yeah, I know what you mean. A damp cold always brought out Mom's aches and pains, too. One of the reasons they moved to Florida was to get away from winter." The desultory conversation made it seem as if they were old acquaintances. Maybe even friends. It was a comfortable feeling, something Tucker couldn't remember experiencing with a woman in a long time. Maybe never.

"We've got to think of something. A wet cement block motel is hardly the most hospitable environment for an elderly arthritic woman and a man who's a semi-invalid."

"Harold's no invalid, semi or otherwise. Don't let that paunch and gray hair fool you, he's in great shape for his age. He square-dances. He takes vitamins."

"So does Bernie. At least she does something called the macaroni. It's this dance where you use your body more than your feet. Which is perfect for someone who has foot problems."

The look he sent her over the bucket of chicken expressed his thoughts with painful clarity, and Annie plucked at a loose thread on her sleeve. "Look, regardless of whether or not we approve, they have a right to live their own lives. I'm beginning to feel a bit mean-spirited about the whole thing."

Tucker sighed. The windshield had steamed up on the inside, creating the illusion of intimacy. "Yeah, me too. It's Jay I ought to be worrying about. I've got a feeling he's pretty mixed up about a lot of things."

"I know how that can be."

"You ever had a teenage son with dyslexia, hyper-something-or-other, plus a bunch of other labels? In my day, it was just part of growing up. Kids had more energy than a barrelful of monkeys, but nobody expected them to act like small adults. Nowadays...I

don't know.'' He shook his head. "Seems like nobody's just your average, everyday, hell-raising, into-
everything-but-homework kid anymore.''

"I've got some books that might help.''

"I've read books. All they did was try and ration-
alize kid behavior into something they could prescribe
a pill for. You think maybe it's a conspiracy?'' He
leaned forward to clear a place on the windshield, and
Annie was momentarily distracted by the way his
sleeve strained over his shoulders, his khakis over his
muscular thighs.

"I suspect it's more likely a combination of guilt
and technology. Children born into today's high-tech
society are almost a different species. I'm beginning
to feel like a dinosaur.''

"Yeah, well:…Jay still likes fishing better than anything else. That's pretty low-tech.'' Tucker stroked
his jaw, and Annie stared at his hand. He had nice
hands. Square palms, with long, straight fingers and
suprisingly well-kept nails. "Know what I think?'' he
said thoughtfully.

"I'm afraid to ask.''

He grinned suddenly, looking entirely too attractive
for Annie's peace of mind. "Saved by the bell. Here
they come.''

Just in time, too, she told herself, trying not to be
too disappointed. The atmosphere inside the steamy
pickup truck was beginning to be a little too intimate
for safety.

He helped her down and reached inside for the
chicken while Annie brushed the wrinkles from her
old camel-tan polo coat and tried to catch her breath.

You'd think she'd never been touched by masculine hands before. My mercy, he wasn't even handsome. If there was a speck of softness on him anywhere, it didn't show. Yet she had to admit he was rather attractive, once you got past the blunt features and those deep-set hazel eyes.

The trouble with you, Annie Summers, is that you're suffering from neglect. And maybe from exposure to too many of Bernie's raunchy posters, too much of her MTV, too many of her soap operas.

Or maybe too little.

They didn't stay long. They didn't even open the chicken, because Harold had brought corn dogs, fries and fried apple pies for two, and they were all set to watch a movie on TV. Something about cowboys and angels.

"It's just awful," Annie whispered once they were outside again. "I could cry for them."

"Cut loose, if you think it'll help." Tucker turned up the collar of his bomber jacket and guided her past a large puddle. He was carrying the bucket of chicken, which was stone cold by now.

"The place smells," she wailed softly.

"It stinks."

With a little hiccup that was part laughter, part sob, she said, "Grammatically, you're right. The thing is, what are we going to do about it? Bernie's not used to living like that."

"Harold's lived in Florida for the past seven years. Sunshine, shuffleboard, seafood and fresh air."

"Right now I'd settle for any one of the above.

Well, maybe not the shuffleboard, I've never been particularly athletic.''

"Honey, I don't think shuffleboard falls into that category.''

"Then maybe I should try it.''

He'd called her "honey.'' When was the last time a man had called her honey? Not that it meant anything, but on a day like this, with no sunshine and no answers in sight, it helped.

"Have you had supper?''

"Not yet.''

"Me, either. Could I interest you in cold chicken?''

She was tempted, oh, so tempted. "I've got reams of paperwork waiting to be done.''

"Yeah, me, too. Reckon I'd better drop you and the chicken off and get started.''

She'd been about to ask if he'd like to share the chicken and maybe a large salad. Bad idea. Really, really bad idea. What she had to do required concentration, and Tucker Dennis was becoming a rather large distraction.

Late that night Annie sat in the parlor rocker listening to the old house creak and groan as the temperature dropped into the mid-forties. She wanted Eddie to come home. She'd even settle for Bernie and her inane TV shows and her ice cream and popcorn and soda cans left for Annie to collect every night before bedtime. This was what it would feel like without Eddie. Without anyone to share the rest of her life. Empty. Lonely.

But it wasn't Eddie her thoughts lingered on, it was Tucker Dennis.

Across town, Tucker tried to focus on the late news. He tried to find the energy to get up and go dish up a bowl of ice cream, but it wasn't there. Neither the energy nor the interest.

It was too late to call Jay. Too late to call Harold. Annie?

Oh, hell, no. What would be the point in that?

Three days later there wasn't a cloud in the sky. The temperature soared into the high fifties and forsythia burst out like golden fireworks against a winter-drab background.

And Bernie's cat disappeared.

Actually, he might have disappeared before that, only Annie had been too wrapped up in this Bernie-Harold business, along with the usual hassles at school, to notice that his dollar-ninety-eight can of salmon hadn't been touched and his milk bowl had collected a film of dust on the top.

The spring term was in session, bringing a fresh batch of problems. One of the temps quit without giving notice, which left Annie trying frantically to find a substitute for the substitute. It seemed there was a serious shortage of substitute teachers. She wondered if it would help to issue a mandate forbidding any teacher to get pregnant during the school year.

At any rate, Zen, that wretched creature, was gone and she hadn't even noticed his absence.

The phone was ringing when she let herself in. She grabbed it while she dumped her briefcase and shed her coat, thinking longingly of a cup of tea. "Hey, Annie, it's me—Tucker. Have you heard anything from the honeymooners in the past couple of days?"

"No, have you? I've been so busy I haven't had time to worry, and now the cat's missing."

"Beg pardon?"

"Bernie's cat. I dislike him intensely, but I'd hate for something bad to happen to him." Unless I did it, she added silently, smothering her guilt.

"Uh…yeah. Well, I just wondered if you'd heard anything."

"No, have you?"

"Not in a day or two. Want to drive out and check on them?"

Annie gnawed on a hangnail. "I need to look for Zen. I thought he'd be waiting on the back steps by the time I got home. I'd better find him before I talk to Bernie again."

"Right. Well…I just thought I'd check in."

He didn't hang up. Neither did she. After a long pause, which was, surprisingly, not uncomfortable, Tucker said, "Annie, you sound tired."

"It happens occasionally when one is shut up in a madhouse all day."

"Yeah, I guess that'd do it, all right," he said, sounding every bit as tired as she felt. She wondered what the situation was with his son, decided she didn't need to know and would be better off not getting any more personally involved with the Dennises than she already was.

In over her head, in other words.

"You still there?"

She murmured that she was. It was as if neither of them had anything to say, yet neither of them wanted to break the connection. Annie finally did, and wondered afterward as she sipped her tea, then put on a pair of old mud walkers and let herself out the back door, if Tucker could've had another reason for calling.

Maybe he'd learned something and didn't know how to tell her. About what that pair was planning.

Oh, Lord, as if she didn't have enough to worry about. "Zen! You wicked old slob, come here! Kitty, kitty, kitty? Come on, please—you need your supper and I need a good hot soak."

Before she was even dressed the next morning, Tucker was on the phone. "Did you find the cat?"

"No. Have you heard anything?"

"About the cat? No, but I wondered—is he neutered?"

"How would I know, he's not my cat. I meant about Bernie and Harold."

"I know for a fact Harold's not neutered. Okay, okay, I'm sorry. Matter of fact I got a call first thing this morning."

"Tucker, this *is* the first thing this morning."

"Oh. Yeah. I'm an early riser."

Annie shifted her weight, tightened her bathrobe sash and glanced at the wag-tailed clock on the wall. It was twelve past seven. "What did you learn?"

"Look, why don't we get together after work today. It's nothing that can't wait till then."

"Is either of them sick?"

"Negative."

"In trouble with the law?"

"Not so far as I know." He chuckled, and the sound went a long way toward making up for her lack of breakfast.

"Then you're right, it can wait."

"Fine. What time do you get home after school?"

She told him. It wasn't as early as she'd have liked, but there was always more to do than any one person could fit into an eight-hour day. She had the usual round of errands on the way home. Bank, supermarket, bookstore.

"I'll be by with pizza about seven. What do you like on yours?"

"How do you know I like pizza at all?"

"Everybody likes pizza."

"Wholewheat crust, extra cheese, no meat, broccoli, bell peppers, onions?"

"You expect me to go in there and ask for something like that?"

"I've got chilli." She had two cartons of vegetarian chili left in the freezer, enough for two hungry people.

"Is that an invitation?"

She closed her eyes and took a deep breath. "Yes, I guess it is."

Annie hung up the phone and thought, what on earth am I doing?

Not that it was a dinner date. It was more like a conference. A trouble-shooting session. Still, he was coming here for supper, and they would talk about

Bernie and Harold, and maybe go on to talk about a few more topics like his son, and her—

Her what? Her wildly exciting career as an assistant principal? Her fiancé's wildly exciting career doing whatever it was he did, which was probably a lot more interesting than what she did, only she wasn't quite sure what it was.

Or if she even had a fiancé any longer.

"Face it, Annie, you have about as much to offer an attractive single man as that hat rack out in the hall."

And yes, the man was attractive. She might be practically on the shelf, but she wasn't yet moribund. Tucker Dennis, whatever else he was, was incredibly sexy in his worn work clothes and those big, clunky boots. Engineer boots, she'd heard them called. He wasn't the type to wear cowboy boots. Too showy. He was more the unpretentious what-you-see-is-what-you-get type.

"Don't even think about it, Annie Summers. You have a problem in common, and that's *all* you have in common. Forget that at your peril."

Five

Tucker shoved back his bowl after the second serving of chili and belched discreetly. "That was pretty good," he said, not even trying to hide his surprise. When he'd found out that the meat wasn't meat, but a bunch of chopped-up vegetables and soy beans, he'd nearly backed out, but it had smelled good. Besides, she'd baked corn bread, and he'd always been a sucker for corn bread. Hers was a damn sight better than the mix he'd tried the last time Jay had come home. She served it with molasses and something called tahini. He didn't even want to know what was in that.

"So...ready to get down to brass tacks?"

"I made coffee. I don't usually, but I thought you'd prefer it to strawberry tea."

It was weak, stale and decaffeinated, but he was too polite to mention it. His mama had taught him a few manners, after all. A man living alone, or in purely masculine company, tended to let such things slide.

"So...you got any good ideas up your sleeve?" It was a nice sleeve. Blue. Softer than cotton, thinner than wool. Maybe silk?

Nah. Not silk. Not on Annie Summers. She probably thought silk was the devil's invitation to sin.

"You're the one who wanted to talk," she reminded him.

"Right. Well, the way I see it, the motel's cheap, but it's not free. Harold's check is still a couple of weeks off, so unless he's cashed in his mutuals or your cousin's bought herself a winning lottery ticket, they can't afford to stay there much longer. What now? Are you going to take them in, or am I?"

"Oh, now wait as minute—"

"Because I'll warn you right now, I run an all-male operation. Me and my Dad. And Jay, between school, camp and whatever else my ex-wife dreams up to keep us apart."

She took a few minutes to digest that. Tucker watched the awareness grow. A slight frown gathered between her brows, and she removed her glasses and tried to rub it away.

"There's no law that says you can't take in a mother-in-law," she said. He started to protest, but she plowed doggedly ahead. "A second-cousin-in-law is something else. There are limits to how many people I can take in without being accused of running a boarding house. Besides, my fiancé's mother is practically packed and waiting to move in as soon as Eddie and I are married. She's not at all happy where she's living now.''

''Fiancé, huh?''

''She has a dog—a chow. With Bernie's cat, it's not going to work. And then there's your father's pipe. Rosa—that's Eddie's mother—has allergies.''

''God help her if she gets a whiff of Bernie's perfume.''

''I know.'' She sighed. It was as if the wind had suddenly gone right out of her sails. ''What on earth are we going to do, Tucker? We have to do something.'' Her shoulders drooped. She sagged back against the chair, long legs extended out in front of her, crossed at the ankles.

And Tucker, distracted because it was the first time she'd called him by his given name, thought, yeah— it had to be silk. Nothing else slithered over a woman's body the way silk did. ''Hey, don't give up on me now. We'll come up with something if we put our minds to it. Now, the way I see it—''

''Zen.''

''Zen. Right. Whatever you want to call it. Anyhow, the way I see it, if we put our heads together, we ought to be able to come up with a solution.''

Her head was back. Her eyes were closed. Tucker took the opportunity to study the stranger who had unexpectedly become a part of his personal life. He watched the pulse beating at the side of her throat and tried to think of what her skin reminded him of. Mozarella cheese didn't quite do it justice, but it came close. Soft, but firm. Smooth, pale…

Nobody had ever accused him of being romantic. "Annie?" he ventured.

"What?"

"Hey, are you okay?"

"You mean aside from a lost cat that I'll have to either find or explain? A fiancé I haven't seen since last Easter or heard from since Christmas? A potential mother-in-law who keeps asking if she should renew her lease for another three months? Oh, and what about a runaway cousin? What about two bald tires that need replacing and a prescription that needs changing that I can't fit into my budget?" She waved a hand over her eyes. "Oh, Lord, I'm whining. I *hate* whiners."

Tucker resisted the urge to wrap her in his arms and rumple her hair, the way he used to do with Jay when the going got a little too tough. Fortunately, before he could land any deeper in trouble, his orderly engineer's brain kicked in. "Your trouble is perspective. What you need to do is back off, look at the broad picture, and then set your priorities. Number one, your prescription. Screw up your health and the rest won't matter. I don't want to know the details of your budget, but if you need a loan, I can—"

"Oh, for heaven's sake, it's nothing like that." She waved a languid hand at him. "It's just that my short vision's getting longer and my long vision's getting shorter. I keep hoping they'll meet in the middle and I can throw away my glasses, but until that happens…"

Well, hell—what could he say to that? His eyes were 20/20, just like his dad's. Good eyesight ran in the family.

Might be interesting to find out what ran in hers. Any family that could turn out two women as different as Annie and Bernice Summers must have a pretty weird gene pool.

"Okay, we'll move on to the next item. All the same, if you need help, just—"

She opened her eyes and stared at him. Large gray eyes with delicately arched eyebrows and long, silky brown lashes. If she wore any makeup, it didn't show. A face like hers—what you might call classic—didn't really need any enhancement.

"If we're going to be organized about this business," she said, "then the cat should probably come first."

"Before the fiancé and the mother-in-law?"

"Without a husband, I won't have a mother-in-law, and there's not much I can do about Eddie at the moment. He's off on another save-the-world mission where telephones are few and far between. Evidently that goes for mail service, too."

Tucker knew for a fact that in these days of satellite communications, few places on the globe were truly inaccessible. "Okay, the cat then. Last known sighting?"

"Um…yesterday. Maybe the day before, I'm not sure. I've had a lot on my mind lately."

"No kidding."

She bit her lip, but a few of the shadows left her eyes. "All right, I'm a dreadful person, I admit it. But if anything happens to Zen, Bernie's going to be heartbroken. She's had him for nearly thirteen years."

"Have you asked around the neighborhood?"

"Not yet."

"Seems like the logical place to start."

"I know."

"So?"

"So I hate that cat. I really hate him, and I assure you, the feeling's mutual. He's gone into hiding, sulking because Bernie's deserted him. He likes to see us suffer."

"Cats don't have human emotions."

"Bernie's cat does. Malice is a human emotion."

"So is guilt, but you don't need to feel guilty just because you don't happen to like a particular animal. Me, I hate parrots."

She looked at him in disbelief. "Nobody hates parrots, they're birds. Besides, they're gorgeous."

"You've never had your nose nearly amputated by an Amazon you were offering a peanut to, right? Believe me, it makes a lasting impression."

A smile dawned in her eyes, then trembled on her lips. Tucker cleared his throat and said, "Yeah, well...I guess we'd better look for your cat. Maybe you can board him out until we can think of a way to pry those two out of that damned Blue Flamingo."

"You really do have a thing against birds, don't you?" She bit back a smile.

Tucker tried not to notice how her eyes seemed to glow when she was amused. "Have you considered bribery?"

"Bribery, blackmail, arson, kidnapping, calling the sheriff."

"Who for? The cat or Bernie?"

"I tried bribery on the cat, but it didn't work. I haven't tried it on Bernie yet." She closed her eyes and smiled again, and Tucker got sidetracked by the difference a smile made. He nearly missed what she said next. "Bernie reads *Penthouse*."

"You're kidding. That old—that—*Bernice?*"

"She says it has good articles."

"Right. That's like pleading the fifth."

"Probably. Anyway, I don't think blackmail will work, and I draw the line at kidnapping and arson. I'm not even sure if cement blocks would burn. Do you suppose if we asked them point-blank, they might tell us what they're planning to do?" Annie opened her eyes reluctantly. They ached. Her head ached. She'd like to lay the blame on Bernie and that wretched cat of hers, but it was probably a result of her own overworked, astigmatic eyes.

"Can't hurt to try. Once we find your cat and get our respective relatives sorted out, we'll tackle your fiancé and his mother and—what was the next one?"

"Forget it. It's my problem. Not your father, but the rest of it." She sat up, drew her feet up onto the rungs of the rocker and leaned forward, arms on her knees, head in her hands.

Tucker had taken the massive recliner her father had bought when they'd furnished the house. Large, leather covered, it was a man's chair. Eddie had sat in it only once. He'd looked utterly lost, but then, Eddie was slender and only an inch taller than she was. He'd always reminded her of a young, blond Sinatra, although lately, she had to study his picture to remember what he looked like. Even so, his image was beginning to fade.

Tucker, on the other hand, looked right at home in the massive chair. He was a big man. Tonight he was wearing starched and creased khakis, obviously just back from the laundry, a dark flannel shirt and a baggy tweed jacket. He was freshly shaved, and she'd caught a whiff of some crisp, light scent. A far cry from the motorcycle-riding, blue-jeans-wearing barbarian who had nearly run her down at the Blue Flamingo a little over a week ago.

Although there was still that air of steely masculine determination.

Otherwise known as stubborn male pigheadedness. Tonight he was on his good behavior.

"About Zen," she said tiredly. "Do you have a plan?"

"Why don't you start calling?"

"I've called until I'm hoarse. He ignores me."

"I meant on the phone. To see if anyone's seen him. I'll go outside and whistle a few times. If you don't count parrots, I'm usually pretty good with animals."

She gave him a flashlight, which he said he didn't need. She told him cats' eyes were chatoyant, and that a light might help.

"Cha-*what?*" He gave her a strange look and shook his head, but took the flashlight and stuck it in his hip pocket.

Under the pink glow of a sodium vapor streetlight,

she watched him lope down the back stairs like a lifeguard on one of those shows Bernie loved to watch.

What on earth has happened to your mind, woman? You're ogling!

Back in the kitchen, she called every house on the block. The block was large, but so were the yards and houses. There weren't all that many. The Rappoports were on vacation. None of the others had seen a strange cat.

And then she stood in the back door and listened while Tucker alternately whistled and crooned. "Here, kitty, kitty, kitty. Come on, you damned flea-bitten critter, don't you know you're too old to be out tomcatting? C'mere, kitty. C'mere, Zen."

Annie made another pot of coffee and wished she had something to offer for dessert. Fruit suited her just fine, but she had an idea Tucker might be used to something a bit richer. "Maybe I should just go ahead and tell Bernie her cat's missing," she said after he'd given up and come inside again. "She might even decide to come home and look for him herself. Want some graham crackers?"

"Might be worth a try."

"Telling Bernie, or the graham crackers?"

"Bernie and the cat. Better your house than mine."

Annie held up a hand, palm out. "Now hold on, I'm not planning to take in both of them."

"You're going to make her choose between her husband and her cat?"

He helped himself to a handful of graham crackers while Annie jammed her fists into her pockets, hoping the seams would bear the strain. The fabric was called silk denim, which was a contradiction in terms, not that anyone these days paid the least attention to things like that. "One problem at a time, all right? I'll give the cat one more day to come home, and then I'll tell Bernie and see what she wants to do about it, and go from there."

"Right. Ready to move on to the next problem?" Still in the kitchen, his hips braced against the countertop, he reached for another graham cracker, started to dunk it in his coffee and changed his mind.

"Go ahead, dunk if you want to."

He looked at her, looked at the cracker and shook his head. "Graham crackers lack the tensile strength for good dunking. Now, as I see it," he said thoughtfully, "we need to come up with a plan, plus a few alternative plans in case our newlyweds prove stubborn."

She faked a sweet smile. "Stubborn? I think that's what's called a given. Do you get the feeling they're up to something?"

His eyebrows shot up. They were nice eyebrows, thick, but well groomed. "You mean besides—well, the usual honeymoon fun and games?"

"Oh, for heaven's sake, Bernie's seventy-one. Your father must be even older than that."

"So? What's your point?"

"Well, I just thought—I mean, obviously—"

"I didn't see a deck of cards or a checkerboard, did you?"

"No, but—well, surely…"

"Look, their personal life is their business. What you and I have to deal with is—"

Annie placed a jar of organic peanut butter and a knife on the table beside him. "I thought you were every bit as opposed to this match as I am. Was I wrong about that? Did I misunderstand when you called my cousin a—a—brass-plated mantrap?"

"Brass-headed." He held up a placating hand. "Look, we're beyond that, all right? They're married, they're of age, they're entitled. It's the logistics we have to work out. They have to live somewhere. You don't want Dad here because he happens to smoke a pipe occasionally, but I live in a five-room dump out in the sticks. A woman like Bernie would be climbing the walls in no time. Women like to live in town, in big houses, with country clubs and shopping malls in easy reach."

Annie stared at him until a tide of ruddy color crept up past his collar. They both knew that in that one statement, he'd said far more about his own marriage than he'd intended. Or that she had any desire to know.

She mentioned the zoning laws. "I know they're family—at least Bernie is, but you see, one of my neighbors recently got into trouble by inviting half a dozen so-called relatives to move in. For a price. The zoning board's been watching the whole neighborhood like a hawk ever since."

"Yeah, well, like I said, my place is too small. It's not that I have anything against Bernie personally, but—" Annie made a rude sound at that. "Well, hell, I don't even know her. She's probably a real nice lady, but her perfume is strong enough to drive the roaches out of the cracks, and Jay's coming home pretty soon and—''

''So? What's your point?'' Annie threw his own challenge back at him. They stared at each other for one long moment and then burst into laughter. Both of them. For Annie, it was more like hysterical release. She didn't know what it felt like for Tucker, but it looked good and it sounded good, and suddenly none of her problems seemed quite so overwhelming.

He left a few minutes later, promising to sleep on it and give her a call the next day. ''At which time,'' he said as he brushed past her at the front door, ''we'll tackle the next few items on your list. The missing fiancé, the threat of a mother-in-law invasion and—what's next? Tires? Glasses? You name it, we'll find an answer. Least I can do since we're family now.''

''We're *what?*''

''Cousins-in-law?''

''Loose connections, at the very most,'' she said repressively. ''*Temporary* loose connections.''

On the wide front porch, he turned and lifted a hand in careless salute. Annie watched him stride down the front walk and wondered what there was about the man that made him so impossible to ignore.

Family?

No way. There was something going on here, but for the life of her, she couldn't figure out what it was.

They weren't really family. On the other hand, they weren't really friends. Which left...

"Don't ask. Don't even think about it," she muttered, and slammed the door hard enough to rattle the beveled-glass panels.

Six

Tucker put off facing the problem of what to do about Harold and Bernice as long as possible the next day. His morning had begun with a call from Jay's school counselor. It seemed that things weren't quite as rosy as Tucker had been led to believe. In spite of all those glowing building-confidence-and-self-esteem reports, Jay's grades, except for math, were down the tubes.

Scowling, he got out the makings for a lunch-to-go. Peanut butter and jelly. Halfway through scraping the bottom of the peanut butter jar he had a call from Dean Barger, friend and codeveloper of Half Moon Properties, who'd been having marital problems.

"Man, Tuck, she's lost it. I mean, last night, she pitched a fit you wouldn't believe!"

Tucker's advice was short and pointed. "Next time you go out of town on a business trip, take her along."

"Hell, man, I can't do that. A wife would only cramp my style."

"Maybe your style needs cramping. If I remember correctly, you two made some promises when you got married." Tucker had been best man at the wedding. "Has she been running around on you?"

"Ah, you know Jeannine, she's not like that, man."

"But you are, right? So it's okay for you to cheat, but not for your wife. Why don't you think about that for a while, and see if you can find any holes in the logic."

He was on his way to the truck when the house phone rang again. Turning back, he unlocked the front door just as the machine kicked in, and heard the contractor who was supposed to have finished the paving on the last section a week ago saying he wouldn't be able to wind it up until early next month, as his wife's mother up in Utah was having gall bladder surgery.

He swore under his breath. Then, before he could escape again, Harold called, wanting to know if his check had arrived.

"Dad, it's only the twenty-seventh of the month."

"Thing is, Son, this outfit insists on being paid by the week, and I'm running a little short."

"Didn't I hear somewhere that two could live as cheaply as one? Was that just one of those crazy rumors?"

"Sounds like it. I guess you know more than I do about money and wives," Harold observed dryly.

Tucker did. It didn't improve his mood. "Look, I'll drop by later on today with a check, okay?"

"Whenever it's convenient. And, Son—cash would be better."

"Fine. Cash, then," he snapped.

And regretted his sharpness when Harold said quietly, "I really appreciate this, Son. I know I've put you to a lot of trouble, but I'll try not to worry you again."

Talk about your guilt trips. Tucker couldn't begin to count the times the old man had hauled his butt out of trouble, dusted him off and set him back on track, without once blowing his stack.

Feeling as if he were being squeezed between two generations, each determined to wear him down, he called Annie, desperately needing a dose of that cool composure that was so characteristic. Wet, tired, or mad as hell, she usually managed to sound as if she had everything under control.

The funny thing was, Tucker had always hated it when a woman refused to blow up when the occasion called for it. Shelly had been like that. He'd be spoiling for an argument. She'd file her nails. He'd threaten to cut up her credit cards, she'd yawn and tell him to go ahead, she had other cards she hadn't even broken in yet.

In Shelly's case, it had been a combination of two things—immaturity and a lack of caring.

In Annie's case...

He hadn't quite figured out what it was with Annie,

but he'd lay odds is was neither immaturity nor a lack of caring. She would let herself go just so far, and then that control would switch on and she'd walk away, leaving him wanting to spit a few nails.

"Hey, Annie, it's me—Tucker Dennis. Look, it's time we settled this business with Harold and Bernie once and for all," he said tightly.

"Have you heard anything?"

"Only that they're about to get tossed out on their ear unless I come up with the ransom."

"Mercy, are you serious?"

"About halfway. I guess I'm blowing off steam."

"I use Mozart and strawberry tea."

"Are we talking about the same thing?"

"Stress. You sound terribly stressed."

He took a deep breath, avoided the temptation to tell her just how stressed he was and said instead, "Something's got to give. How about we meet at that steak house out near the motel after work? We can have supper and decide on a plan of action."

"Is it really necessary? I had plans for the evening."

"It's necessary. Look, if you've got a date, I'll handle things myself. You might want to get a room ready, though."

"No, wait—"

"No problem. I wouldn't want to interfere with your social life. But make up your spare room before you go out, just in case."

"Oh, for heaven's sake, I'll postpone my plans. Before you do anything drastic, we need to talk about it."

"That's what I said. Your place, my place, or neutral territory?"

"Neutral territory, by all means."

"Right. The steak house, then. I have to run out to the motel later on, anyway. Might as well make one trip do for all."

"I suppose."

She didn't sound any too thrilled at the prospect, but hell—neither was he. "Look, we're in this thing together, so until it's settled we might as well make an effort to keep the peace. I'll pick you up about six, okay?"

"I'd rather meet you there."

"No point in both of us driving."

In the ensuing silence, he could practically hear her mind working, trying to come up with an excuse to back out.

Strawberry tea and Mozart? What the hell kind of a woman was she? He was tempted to suggest that beer and Waylon Jennings might be more effective, but then, neither had worked too well in his case.

"All right, then, I'll meet you at the restaurant at six if you insist," she said, and before he could react, she hung up.

If *he* insisted? If he remembered correctly, he'd offered to pick her up. *She'd* been the one to insist on her own wheels.

On the other hand, he'd been the one to press for the steak house, while she claimed she'd had a date. Hadn't she?

For the life of him, he couldn't figure out who'd won this particular round.

Tucker was early. All day long he'd dealt with the usual hassles without blowing his cool, possibly because his brain was only about half-involved. At ten of five he'd locked up and raced home, showered, shaved and changed into fresh jeans, a dress shirt, a necktie Jay had given him last Father's Day, and his old tweed jacket.

Hell, he'd even splashed on a palmful of cologne. He'd felt like a fool the minute he'd done it, but the stuff wouldn't wipe off, and he didn't have time to shower a second time.

Rather than sit and stew when he saw that her car wasn't there, he drove a few miles down the highway, pulled over and gazed out across a broad, rolling pasture edged with hedgerows. Waiting for the stress that was a constant companion to ease, he visualized the field dotted with two-bedroom houses and decided he much preferred it the way it was.

After about ten minutes he took a deep breath and flexed his shoulders a few times. Then, watching for traffic, he made an illegal three-point turn in the middle of the highway and drove back to the restaurant.

Annie's beige sedan was among the dozen or so cars there. Tucker pulled into the slot beside her. Her head was back, her eyes closed. He knew the feeling.

So as not to startle her, he rapped on the glass, then opened her door and held out his hand to assist her for no reason other than that she was that kind of a woman. He'd have done the same for his mother, and God knows, Annie didn't remind him of his mother.

Cousin-in-law? No way. He had a couple of cousins. One was a court stenographer with the face of an angel and the body of a sumo wrestler. The other worked for the Justice Department in Raleigh. Neither of them bore the slightest resemblance to Annie Summers.

"Sorry I'm late," he lied.

"That's all right. Did you notice how long the days are getting? I enjoyed sitting here watching the sky change."

"You were sound asleep," he teased.

"Then it was a lovely dream."

There it was again. That unflappable way she had of dealing with whatever came along. She'd slipped out of character once or twice with this Bernie and Harold thing, not to mention the cat, but he'd lay odds it would take a lot more than a missing cat and a surprise elopement to really rattle her cage.

It was beginning to bother him, the way he knew in advance how she'd react to a given situation. He had never known anyone even faintly like Annie Summers, yet he felt as if he'd known her forever. Without ever discussing the weightier things in life, such as religion, politics, baseball, music—not necessarily in that order—he sort of knew where she'd line up. He knew she took her responsibilities seriously. They had that much in common.

He knew, or rather he suspected, that in spite of her fiancé, in spite of the fact that she worked with people all day and shared her home with a relative, she was lonely.

So was he.

And he was scared stiff that if either of them ever admitted it, they'd end up doing something they would both come to regret. Because underneath all this other stuff, there was a glowing spark that had nothing to do with Harold or Bernie, nothing to do with missing cats or absent fiancés or problem sons. Whatever it was, it was dangerously physical. What's more, he was all but certain it was mutual. A man could tell about these things.

He'd even caught her looking him over a time or two in a way that wasn't altogether disinterested. He wondered if she knew just how revealing clear, gray eyes could be.

Maybe he ought to warn her he wasn't in the market for anything too heavy. Didn't have time. Even if he had time, Annie Summers wouldn't be a candidate. Annie wasn't a part-time woman. As evidence, there was this guy she was supposed to be engaged to. A package deal, mother-in-law included.

Hell of a deal, if you asked him, but there it was. The responsibility thing. First a second cousin, then a mother-in-law. No way was he going to get mixed up with a woman carrying that kind of baggage. He had enough of his own.

All the same, a guy couldn't help but speculate....

"So. What'll it be, T-bone, sirloin or strip?" he asked, hoping she hadn't got a whiff of his cologne.

Hoping she wasn't tuned in on his wavelength.

"Mmm, could I have a baked potato and a salad?"

"Sure, order as many sides as you want." He took her coat and admired the way the blue silk moved over her trim rear end when she walked.

What she wanted was baked potato and salad. Period.

"Ever hear of anemia? Iron deficiency?"

"Ladies take tonics," she said with barely a glint in those solemn gray eyes of hers.

"Right. And men chew nails." He grinned and got an answering smile, which was worth the guilt he was probably going to feel, sitting across the table feasting on a slab of rare beef while she daintily picked at her vegetables.

Over dessert they got down to business. "I was only kidding about your guest room. Way I figure it, they can pool their social security and just about swing a place—maybe an apartment, maybe even a small fixer-upper. But what about all the rest?"

"You're speaking of food, transportation, not to mention medical and dental. Even with medicare, that can eat a hole in anyone's budget."

"Yeah, I know. Dad's still covered under the company's group policy. I guess Bernie's eligible now, too, but it's still a pretty hefty co-pay."

They both frowned. Annie gazed at the salt shaker. Tucker gazed at Annie. After a while he said, "Dad could probably get a break on the rent if they could find a small fixer-upper. There's nothing he can't build or repair. I could have my guys lend a hand with the plumbing, electrical, that sort of thing."

"I wonder if Bernie's told him yet that she hates cooking and housework."

"Harold doesn't mind pitching in. There's always takeout. TV dinners. Frozen pizzas. I doubt if they'll starve."

"I could take something over to them two or three

times a week. Maybe a Crock-Pot of black bean soup or vegetarian chili and a pan of corn bread.''

Tucker forgot what she was saying as he watched the play of expression on her pale, oval face. Classic. Yeah, that was it. Like those famous old paintings of barefooted ladies draped in curtains, with their hair hanging down past their behinds. Only skinnier.

"People are so different," she said with a sigh. "Politicians are always telling you what the American people want, as if the.American people were a homogeneous blob. The truth is, they want different things. I haven't a clue what Bernie wants from this marriage, much less what your father's expecting. Or what either of them is willing to put into it." She reached out and lifted a limp French fry from his plate and absently nibbled on it, a clear indication of just how distracted she was.

How much effort, he wondered, would someone like Annie be willing to put into a marriage? Some women—his ex-wife came to mind—were takers. Didn't know how to be anything else. He had an idea Annie was different, but then, he hadn't recognized Shelly's inherent selfishness and immaturity until it was too late.

Some lessons had to be learned the hard way. The painful way.

On the other hand, without Shelly, there wouldn't be Jay, and Jay was worth any amount of pain and disillusionment.

Tucker insisted on paying for their dinner. Annie protested, but didn't make an issue of it. He suggested they take one car and leave the other one here, but she insisted on driving herself to the Blue Flamingo.

"Hog-on-ice syndrome, huh?"

"If by that you mean I prefer to be independent, then you're right. Would you like a lift?" she asked, tongue firmly in cheek. "You could leave your truck here and pick it up on the way back."

Annie could hardly believe it when he moved around to the passenger side, opened the door and climbed in. "Sure, why not? Like I said before, no point in both of us driving."

She started the car, put it in gear and nothing happened. Tucker glanced pointedly at her parking brake and she quickly released it, feeling embarrassed and irritated at the same time. "Thanks," she muttered, suppressing an irrational urge to swear.

Heaven alone knew why, but she was finding it increasingly difficult to maintain her composure. Not that she felt threatened. At least she didn't think she felt threatened.

Oh, no? Then why did a shrill voice inside her head keep warning, *Danger. High voltage. Keep out!*

"We still haven't come up with a plan of action," she reminded a few minutes later, pulling into the motel parking lot.

"I thought we'd decided to look around for something affordable, maybe somewhere in your neighborhood."

"Mine?"

"Hey, I live out in the sticks. There's nothing out there but a couple of chicken farms and a fertilizer plant. What about that house you said took in paying guests?''

"Not anymore. The whole neighborhood's zoned single-family residence, even though very few single-families require twelve-room houses these days. Sooner or later that will have to change, with taxes so high and maintenance such a nightmare, but until it does, we're all stuck in a catch-22 situation. The houses are all too old to be practical, not old enough to be historical.''

"Like I said, Harold can repair anything. He'd be handy to have around, and he's family. Since he's Bernie's husband, you won't have any problem with the zoning board. Besides, Harold will insist on paying rent, which will help with the taxes.''

The look he gave her was so patently guileless it might've worked if Annie hadn't known what he was up to. "Smooth," she said dryly. She could've tried the same tactic herself, but while Harold might prove useful in her case, Bernie wouldn't be an asset in either case. She felt like a traitor for thinking such a thing, but there it was. Bernie was useless when it came to keeping house. She was irritating.

For that matter the marriage might not even outlast the honeymoon, in which case each of them could take back their own relative and that would be the end of that.

Oddly enough, the thought wasn't particularly welcome.

They lingered outside under the flickering, blue, headless flamingo sign for several more minutes, reluctant to end the comfortable silence. Annie leaned her head back on the headrest and sighed. "Did you ever wish you could just pack a comb and a toothbrush and walk away? Somewhere—anywhere—no particular goal in mind, just away?"

"A few times. A few hundred times. Trouble is, walking away doesn't solve anything, all your problems are waiting when you come home."

"You sound as if you've actually done it."

Tucker answered after a brief hesitation. "Yeah. I guess you could call it that. Take my word for it, it doesn't work."

"I wouldn't have the courage to do it, even if it did," she said softly, and gave him a wistful smile that hit him where he lived.

The lady was beginning to get under his skin.

He swung open his door and stepped out into the neon-lit parking lot. "Let's go see if we can't sort this business out."

Annie let herself out before he could come around to open her door. Standing beside him in the raw March evening, she said diffidently, "I'm not really looking forward to this, you know."

Tucker rested a hand on her shoulder, and because it felt so right, he left it there as they headed for the honeymoon suite.

"Come on, it won't be all that bad."

Seven

It wasn't all that bad. It wasn't all that good. "I'd call it a draw," Tucker said after saying good-night to the newlyweds some forty-five minutes later.

"But we're right back where we started. I don't think your father even wanted to hear our suggestions."

"What's with your cousin and television?"

"Remember that old show where secret agent Maxwell Smart had a cone of silence? Television is Bernie's cone of silence. Whenever she doesn't want to hear something, she switches it on."

"Every try sending her to her room? Grounding her?"

Tiredly Annie shook her head. "I always thought I was good at dealing with people, but you know something? I'm not. And the worst part of it is that sometimes—a lot of the time lately—I don't even feel like making the effort.''

They had reached her car. Tucker leaned against the door while Annie stood there, hands in her coat pockets, studying the tip of her shoe. Tonight, in honor of impending spring, she was wearing low-heeled tan spectators. Against all reason she'd felt so hopeful when they'd started out this evening.

Although if she were honest with herself, she'd have to admit that part of it—most of it—was simply being with Tucker. Having dinner with him, talking about nothing in particular, they way men and women did when they were skirting around the edges of a relationship of some sort. Testing the waters.

The trouble was, she was beginning to lose sight of the fact that the only relationship she shared with Tucker Dennis involved two other people. Bernie at least had the courage to reach out for something to hold off the loneliness.

Annie had once tried to do the same thing. Now, four years later, all she had to show for it besides nagging calls from a would-be mother-in-law and Eddie's rare letters, which were more like travel-ogues, was more loneliness.

Tucker eased his thumb under her chin to lift her face. ''Hey, it's not so bad. At least we got 'em to thinking about it.''

''I can't believe they haven't considered where they're going to go from here. Not even Bernie is flaky enough to think they can spend the rest of their lives in a motel.''

"I think maybe Harold was waiting for me to suggest something."

"To suggest what?"

He shrugged. "Who knows? Anyhow, once we come up with a suitable place, I'm pretty sure they'll fall into step."

"Any place I consider suitable, Bernie will hate."

"Harold's pretty reasonable."

"That makes one of them."

Tucker studied her face, unnaturally pale in the blinking blue light. He felt the damndest urge to kiss her. To kiss her and wrap his arms around her and tell her everything would be all right.

Mostly he just felt like kissing her.

God, how long had it been since he'd felt like kissing a woman, much less thought about taking her to bed? And he'd thought about it, all right. Too many times lately when he looked at her, the first thought to streak through his mind was, what would happen if a man ever broke through that control of hers?

Would he find passion?

Would he strike any answering sparks?

Was she as curious as he was about what would happen if they forgot about those two in there—forgot about his son and her fiancé—and explored this thing that was beginning to simmer just beneath the surface?

"I suppose we'd better get back to the restaurant before they tow your truck," she said, shifting her face away from his hand. "But thanks for trying."

"Yeah, sure. We'll come up with an answer. It's

not like they're a couple of kids who can't think for themselves.''

''I know, but I feel responsible for Bernie. I'm all she has.''

''Husbands don't count?''

She gnawed on her lower lip. He could tell she was depressed about the whole affair. Well, hell, so was he. The last thing he'd ever expected his father to do was find himself another wife, without even giving him any warning.

But the deed was done. As the preacher would say, for better or for worse. Now all they could do was make the best of it.

Tucker unlocked her door, then went around to the passenger side and let himself in. Trying for a lighter note, he said, ''First time I've let a woman drive me anywhere since I was fifteen years old. The girl I was dating back then was seventeen. She had a license and I didn't.''

''Mercy, you were socially precocious. How did it affect your ego, being driven around by an older woman?''

He chuckled. ''I seem to recall asking her to drive slow so all the guys could see who I was going out with. I guess you could say my ego survived.''

''You sound like the kind of boy my father used to warn me about.''

''Your father was smart. Did you take the warning?''

''Always,'' she murmured, waiting for traffic to pass to take a right turn into the restaurant's parking lot. ''But you know what? Sometimes I wish I'd rebelled, just to see what it felt like.'' She pulled up beside the silver truck with the Dennis Construction logo on the side. Didn't cut the engine, just waited for him to say good-night and get out.

Instead, he reached over and removed the key from the ignition. And then he took her by the shoulders, turned her to face him, leaned across the console and kissed her before she could utter a protest.

By the time Tucker came up for air, his head was reeling, his jeans were about two sizes too small, and he was having trouble with his breathing apparatus. In the pink glare of the parking lot lights, Annie looked dazed. He didn't think it was his technique. If he'd ever had one, it was long since forgotten.

An apology was definitely in order, but the words that came out were, ''Geez, Annie, what are you trying to do to me?''

He'd seen people in shock with that same dazed look. ''Annie? Hey, are you all right?''

''I wasn't—I didn't—''

''Look, I'm sorry. It was a bad idea, okay? I guess I meant it as a joke.''

She looked even more stricken, and he hastened to explain. ''What I meant was, there's no point in complicating an already complicated situation, right?''

''Of course not. I knew that. That it was a joke, I mean. It's already far too complicated. The situation, I mean. Oh, for heaven's sake, I can't even put two words together! Tucker, it's been a long day,'' she ended lamely.

Tucker shifted on the seat, glad the shadow of the dashboard covered him from the waist down. When a guy was wired for 110, he ought to know better than to fool around with 220. Underneath all that insulation, the lady packed a wallop.

"Yeah, for me, too. A long day, that is." He cleared his throat and opened the passenger door. "Look, I'll give it some thought and we'll talk some more tomorrow."

Before she could ask what he was going to be thinking about, he climbed out, shut her door and turned toward his truck.

He knew damned well what he was going to be thinking about, and it wouldn't be prying Harold and his bimbo bride out of the honeymoon suite.

Tucker had planned to wait a couple of days, do some checking around, then call Annie again when he had something to report.

He made it about halfway through the next morning and then called from the office. "It's me, Tucker. You sound winded."

"I've been out searching for the cat again. He's long haired and pretty until you get to know him. Do you suppose someone could've kidnapped him?"

"You might try calling the pound."

"I called. They said they'd let me know if anyone brings in a yellow long-haired male with one white foot."

Neither of them mentioned what had happened the night before. He'd heard about people who believed in a place for everything and everything in its place. That pretty well described Annie Summers's mind. From what he could see she had her whole life laid

out like a post office with walls full of boxes, each
with a number and a lock.

"Look, Annie, about last night—"

"Forget it. I have. It was merely an aberration."

"Is that what it's called? I thought it was merely
a long, hot, wet, sexy kiss."

"Oh, for heaven's sake, we were both tired, at our
wits' end. People sometimes respond to stress by acting on impulse."

"Yeah, well, standing under a cold shower is not
my favorite stress-buster. Maybe I'll try your method.
What was it, strawberry tea and Mozart?" He had a
feeling she was about to hang up on him, and he
didn't want to have to call her back. "Wait a minute,
will you? What I called about was Jay's on his way
home for spring break. I'm meeting him at the airport
in a couple of hours, so I might be pretty busy the
next few days. I've been going over this Bernie-
Harold business, and I think I've come up with a solution."

"That's wonderful. I looked in the classified ads
and couldn't find anything even faintly suitable."

"You remember telling me about your third floor,
and how it's been closed off for years? What if—"

"Oh, no. That's impossible. In the first place,
there's no bathroom up there."

"Not a problem. We can have one in there in three
days, max. I'll supply labor and materials."

"Yes, well—I'd have to get a permit of some sort,
and I probably couldn't. I explained about my neighbor and his trouble with the zoning board, didn't I?"

"Leave all that to me."

"Besides, it's hot as an oven up there in the summertime."

"So we put in a couple of window units."

Between cold showers and the kind of dreams he hadn't had in more than twenty years, Tucker had figured it all out. The sooner they settled the newlyweds, the sooner they could back off and get on with their own lives, before he started getting a few ideas of his own. He'd read somewhere that when men reached a certain age they occasionally pulled some crazy stunt that could really screw up their lives. His father was a perfect example.

"Tucker, I told you about the zoning problem. Look, thanks for trying, but I'm afraid it wouldn't work. I'll think of something."

Totally unflappable, that was Ms. Summers. He'd expected her to bring up his father's cigars. Instead, she just took a deep breath, found one of her little boxes with nothing in it, shoved the loose ends inside and locked the door.

"Like I said, zoning's no problem. We're family, remember?"

"Harold and Bernie are family. You and I are nothing."

"I wasn't planning to move in with you."

"I know that. Of course—well, I suppose…"

Done deal! Tucker silently congratulated himself on shooting down every last one of her objections.

"Of course, there's Bernie's arthritis. All those stairs. Didn't you say yours was a one-story house?"

"Whoa, now hold on a minute."

"If you could run plumbing up to my third floor

and build a bathroom up there, you could easily build a small apartment onto your house.''

''Dammit—''

''I'm sorry, Tucker, I've got to go now. Eddie called and left a message on my machine. He's in New York and will be driving down as soon as he can rent a car and replenish his wardrobe. I have to get a room ready and shop for groceries, and then look for Zen some more. I found a dead mouse on my doorstep this morning. You know what that means.''

She told him goodbye and hung up, leaving him staring at the instrument in his hand. A dead mouse? What the hell was she talking about? And he'd thought *he* was losing it, just because he'd had the kind of dreams last night he hadn't had in more than twenty years.

''No way, lady, you're not getting rid of me that easy.'' Her place wasn't all that far out of the way. He had nearly two hours before Jay's plane was due. He dialed back, and she picked up on the first ring.

''Eddie?''

''No, it's me again. Listen, stay put, will you? I'll be by in about twenty minutes.''

''Oh, but—''

''Annie, it's important. Your guy's not going to be showing up today, is he?''

''No, but—''

''Wait right there.'' He hung up before she could voice any further objections. The lady had too much stiff-necked pride for her own good, but dammit, if some jerk was playing sick jokes on her, pride wasn't going to get the job done.

Annie wondered if thirty-six was too young for menopause. And if menopause could explain palpitations, wakefulness and the kind of erotic daydreams that had gradually disappeared once she'd thrown herself into building a career.

Whatever the reason—whether it was the exposure to a honeymooning couple or exposure to a virile, attractive man—her hormones were definitely acting up. Probably Mother Nature's way of reminding her that she needed to get started on her family if she was ever going to have one. Eddie had promised her as many babies as she wanted, only so far, he hadn't stuck around long enough to get the job done.

"The job? How romantic. Annie, my friend, you're going to have to do better than that," she muttered as she changed out of her gardening clothes into a brown corduroy skirt and beige pullover.

She brushed her hair until it crackled around her face, then pulled it back and twisted it into a coil at the back of her head. Slathered on hand lotion, stared at her image in the mirror, then slowly lifted a hand and touched her lips.

Oh, my mercy. That kiss. If a man's kiss was all that potent, what would it be like to make love with him? Was it different with different men? She knew what making love to a fiancé was like. It was... uncomfortable the first time. Pleasant the second time. A little more pleasant the third time.

There hadn't been a fourth time, because Eddie's

funding had come through and he'd been off on what he'd promised her would be his final adventure before settling down to a teaching position.

By the time Tucker got there, Annie had everything under control. Fresh coffee to be served with biscotti. No more graham crackers that couldn't be dunked because they fell apart. For a woman who'd lived practically all her life without a man, she was learning.

"What's this business about a dead mouse?" It was the first thing he asked her. He looked ready to do battle.

"The mouse? Oh—I thought you understood. It was a gift."

With his brows still lowered in a fierce scowl, he reminded her of one of those grim, battle-weary soldiers who stormed beachheads and crept through jungles on the History Channel. "Look, if someone's playing sick games, Annie, I want you to tell me about it. That kind of thing can get out of hand real fast."

"Tucker, don't you know anything at all about cats?"

"Cats? What do cats have to do with…mice?"

"Right. Cats and mice. They go together like—"

"Hotdogs and baseball."

She looked dubious. "I'll take your word for that. I thought everyone knew about cats and the gifts they brought their people."

"Their people?"

"Well, you can hardly call us their owners. They use us—they taunt us, but I'm sure no one ever really owned a cat. Zen has to be around here, he's only hiding because he knows I'm frantic."

Tucker's shoulders lowered. Some of the starch seemed to go out of him. "Are you frantic, Annie? You don't look frantic, you look cool and composed, like—what is it they say? Like butter wouldn't melt in your mouth?"

"I don't know about butter, but I can think of better ways to start a day than finding a dead mouse on my doorstep, even if it does mean Zen's still in the neighborhood."

There it was again, the Tucker effect. Catches in her breath, a warm feeling as if she were blushing all over. "Tucker, I really appreciate your concern, but I assure you, it's perfectly normal. Don't you know anything at all about cat behavior?"

"Nope. Dogs don't leave their bones lying around, they bury 'em." Evidently he'd raced to the rescue only to find no rescue was needed. Now he was beginning to look embarrassed.

She took pity on him. "Would you care for a cup of coffee before you leave? I suppose you're on your way to the airport."

He glanced at his watch. "Plenty of time. Thanks, I'd like a cup. I finished last week's pot at the office yesterday and never got around to making a fresh pot."

"Last week's pot? The mind boggles."

"So does the stomach."

He followed her into the kitchen, making the spacious room seem suddenly airless. Too close. She took down cups and saucers and reached for one of her seldom-used bread-and-butter plates for the biscotti. The plate was underneath a stack of soup plates, and as she eased it out, the stack shifted. She grabbed for it, and so did Tucker. Together they managed to stave off disaster.

"I've been meaning to clean out these cabinets," Annie said breathlessly. "It's on my list of things to do over the summer."

"Sounds like you've got yourself a dandy vacation planned." He didn't move away. Moved closer, in fact, pinning her against the countertop. There were gold splinters in his eyes. Blue, green, brown and gold. Hazel didn't begin to describe the color.

The plate she was holding slid from her fingers and struck the edge of the huge porcelain sink. Annie blinked and stared down at the three pieces, then reached for the largest piece.

"Let me do that, you'll cut yourself."

"Don't be ridiculous, it's not the first time I've ever broken a dish."

"Annie..." Tucker covered both her hands with his, acutely aware of the difference between his own scarred, callused ones and her long, cool, soft ones. "Annie..."

It was as if a giant vacuum had sucked all the air from the room. His chest felt constricted, his breathing labored. Was this what a heart attack felt like?

"Tucker, are you all right?"

"No. I'm going to kiss you again, Annie, so don't say anything, just let me do it, all right? I need to know if—"

It was every bit as bad as he'd remembered. Worse, in fact. She tasted of strawberries and toothpaste. Felt warm and fragile and strong, and he couldn't get enough of her.

He was in trouble all right. He was so aroused it was painful, and all because of a dead mouse and a broken plate. God knows what would happen if she ever came on to him.

He tilted her head for better access, then took advantage of it. She didn't hold back. After the first startled gasp, she cooperated as if the whole thing had been her idea. Tongues engaged. He savored the taste of her, shuddered when her hands trailed up over his shoulders and brushed against the skin at the back of his neck.

Sliding his hands up under her sweater, he felt the heat of her, the soft strength of her body. Felt it all the way to the marrow of his bones. Then he moved his hands around to cup her breasts. Small, firm, the tips beaded against his palms, shooting streaks of lightning down to his groin.

There was no way in heaven or hell he could keep from grinding his hips against hers. With her mouth open under his assault, he heard her groan, and it was nearly his undoing. Reluctantly—it nearly tore him apart!—he broke away, because it was either that or lower her onto the floor. The table was handy, but it was too short. Looking toward the hall, he was actually thinking of carrying her to the nearest bed when the phone rang.

"Don't answer it," he rasped without opening his eyes.

"It might be Eddie."

You'd think that even if a dead mouse couldn't put a chill on his libido, the mention of her fiancé could.

It didn't. He was still flying the flag when she reached for the kitchen extension and said a breathless "Hello" to whoever was on the other end. "It's Bernie," she whispered.

He opened his eyes. Well, hell. That pretty well did it. His shoulders sagged. So did the rest of him. As for Annie, she had no business looking so damned sexy with her sweater awry and her old-maid topknot sliding down. But then, lust did crazy things to a man's perspective.

Annie tucked the receiver against her breast. "She wants to know about Zen."

"Tell her you'll call her back."

"Bernie, I'll—what? No, I don't hate him.... I did not! Bernie, listen to me—"

She glanced up helplessly at Tucker. "She hung up. She just accused me of hating her cat and hung up."

"Hey, don't take it to heart," he said as she dropped down onto one of the oak straight chairs, plopped her elbow on the table and cupped her chin in her hand.

Feeling as if he'd just run a marathon, Tucker squatted beside her. She refused to look at him. Staring at the refrigerator, she said in a voice that was a little too quiet, a little too controlled considering what they'd been doing, "Honestly, I don't really hate Bernie's cat. I might've said so a time or two, but I didn't mean it. I was only venting."

"Venting. Right."

"We have this mutual antipathy, Zen and I."

"Mutual antipathy. Is that a polite way of saying you hate each other's guts?"

She bit her lip, and he chuckled. And then she did, too. Then both of them stared down at his hand on her knee, and Annie said, "Bernie just doesn't understand that when a cat takes a dislike to someone, he can be truly diabolical. He's brought me mice, lizards, snakes, and once a baby rabbit. They weren't always whole, and they weren't always dead, either."

Tucker was getting a cramp in his left foot from bending it to squat. His football years were ancient history. Now he was paying the toll. "Yeah, I can see how that might be, um—"

"Unpleasant."

"Right. That's the word I was searching for. Annie, would you mind if I got up now?"

She looked at him as if she thought he'd lost his marbles.

"The thing is, I've got this cramp in my foot, and it hurts like hell, and I've got to work it out."

"Oh, well—can I help? For goodness sake, why didn't you say something?"

"I just did." Painfully, but not too awkwardly, he hoped, Tucker stood and pressed his weight against his left foot. He rocked a time or two, flexed what needed flexing, and tried not to think about how foolish he must look. Hell of a follow-up to what just happened. Forty-two years old, and he was falling apart.

"I'm really sorry about this," he said.

"I'm just sorry that—well, there's still coffee. And something for you to dunk. Oh, but I guess you have to get to the airport. Did you have something to tell me first?"

"Something to tell you?"

"About the housing problem?"

"Housing problem?" How the devil was a man supposed to think when his fuse was still smoldering? "Yeah, we're definitely going to have to do something about that. Driving forty-six miles every day gets old real fast."

"How long would it take to build an extension on your house?"

"Don't even think about it. Longer than it would take to add a bathroom to your third floor."

"Bernie's arthritis, remember?"

"Look, I've got to run, and you've probably got things to do to, to get ready for what's-his-name. We can hash it out later."

"Eddie. Edward Henry Robertson."

"Right, Edward."

He headed for the front door, and she followed him, looking worried, sexy and nowhere near as in control of everything as she had when he'd first arrived.

Nowhere near as disheveled as he'd like to see her, either, but that would have to wait for another day.

First there was Jay.

And then Harold and Bernie.

Not to mention what's-his-name. What kind of a

guy went off and left a perfectly good woman alone and unattended?

It would serve him right if someone else snapped her up while he was off doing whatever the hell it was he did.

Eight

Tucker considered several possibilities as he waited for Jay's baggage to come around on the carousel. His son had been kidnapped by space aliens, who had left one of their own in exchange. This kid was someone in the witness protection program who had moved into his son's identity. Or that Shelly had pulled another fast one, only he couldn't figure out how or why, or what it was supposed to accomplish.

Jay—if it was Jay—hadn't said half a dozen words since he'd emerged from the gateway flaunting an orange mohawk, baggy shorts hanging off his skinny butt, with about ten pounds of clunky shoes flapping around his sockless ankles.

"Yo," the boy growled, and scooped a ratty-looking backpack off the conveyor belt.

"How many more do you have?"

His answer was evident in the way the kid looked at him. As if he'd lost his mind or something. Hell, maybe he had. All he knew was that something weird was going on in the airline industry. This was the second time he'd come to the airport to meet a member of his immediate family only to have a stranger turn up in his place. If it weren't for the unusual pale-green eyes from Shelly's side and the Dennis jawline, said to resemble the business end of a bulldozer, Tucker would've walked away, figuring Jay had missed his flight.

They didn't talk much on the way to short-term parking, but not because Tucker didn't give it a try. "Rough term?" he ventured, feeling his way.

"Aaah, you know."

Tucker didn't, but he sure as hell intended to find out. No wonder the kid had needed new waders. His feet must have grown at least a couple of sizes. His face had taken on an angularity that managed to look both belligerent and vulnerable.

"You hungry?" That had never failed him before. Jay could put away more food at a single sitting than a platoon of Marines fresh off maneuvers.

The boy shrugged. His shoulders and feet had grown the most, Tucker decided, which was why the rest of him looked like a wire coat hanger.

"We'll stop on the way home."

That drew another shrug. It also raised Tucker's temper into the red zone, but he tamped it down again. Whatever was going on here, he'd get to the bottom of it. He damned well had to, because somewhere inside the skin of this stranger was a kid he loved so damned much his bones ached with it.

"Talked to your mother lately?"

"Nah." Tucker managed to keep from grabbing the kid by those bony shoulders and shaking the crap out of him. "She's out with this new guy most of the time. I think she's going to marry him or something."

It was the first Tuck had heard of it, but somehow it didn't surprise him. According to his lawyer, the reason Shelly had opted for a huge settlement instead of a more moderate alimony was that alimony stopped if she remarried. She wanted to keep her options open without any financial loss.

"Does it bother you? If your mother remarries, I mean."

"It's cool. Hey, could we go into town on the way home? I need some stuff."

"What kind of stuff?"

"Just stuff. You know."

Tucker didn't know. He did know that one of them was an adult and one of them was a kid, and in his world, adults made the rules.

And then he remembered Harold and the ground rules Tuck and his friends had considered so square. He'd mouthed off once too often, something along the lines of "Get off my back, old man, you don't even know where it's at!" and been grounded for four months, no parole.

Knowing "where it's at" had been important back when he'd been a young rebel. Anti-this, anti-that— convinced that the human brain began to atrophy shortly after the age of twenty-one.

He wondered if Jay knew "where it was at." Or if anyone even used the phrase anymore. No wonder he felt obsolete. By the time he'd finally figured out where it was at, it had moved.

Hell, he couldn't even remember what "it" was supposed to be. He only knew that whatever "it" was, it had passed him by.

Tucker waited until nearly midnight to call, hoping she wasn't asleep. Jay had stayed up long past what used to be his bedtime, stuffing down cold pizza with his head wired up to a boom box. Jimmy Hendrix, for God's sake. What ever happened to those Mormon kids—the Osmonds?

"Annie? Did I wake you up?"

"Tucker? Wha's happened? Are they all right?"

"As far as I know, yeah—everyone's fine. Look, do you have a minute? I'd like to get your take on something." He heard what sounded suspiciously like a yawn at the other end, and could have kicked himself for not thinking before he called. He might've known she'd be the early-to-bed, early-to-rise type.

But then, there was her mysterious fiancé. "Did what's-his-name get there?"

"Where?" She sounded sort of muddled. It was a softer sound than he was used to from Ms. Summers. He liked it. Liked it a little too much.

Clearing his throat, he said, "You know—your fiancé. Didn't you say he was on the way?"

"He is. I guess. And no, he hasn't arrived yet," she said, yawning again.

"Good. I mean, not that it's any of my business,

but with a house guest on the way, I guess you've got plenty to do.''

''Tucker.''

''Making up a guest room—or maybe he won't need one.''

''Tucker, get to the point. Wherever Eddie sleeps, you're right. It's none of your business, so what did you call about? Have you found someplace for the newlyweds?''

''It's about Jay. My son? He'll be fourteen in a couple of months, and I was wondering—I mean, you've had all this experience with adolescents, so I thought…''

''You want my advice on a birthday gift? Tucker, are you out of your mind? I don't even know the child.''

''That's the trouble. Neither do I,'' he muttered. Before he could block out the picture, he saw her lying in bed, the phone cradled in the curve of her long, elegant neck. She'd probably been reading before she fell asleep. Annie was the kind of woman who would read in bed. The kind who didn't plaster her face full of gunk and turn away if someone tried to kiss her good-night.

''Tucker, have you been drinking? In case you haven't noticed, it's the middle of the night. I'm only half a page from the end of the chapter.''

''I knew you'd be reading in bed,'' he said triumphantly. He was tempted to ask what she was wearing, but decided not to push his luck. ''About Jay—what does it mean when a kid that age backs off from questions, doesn't want to talk, doesn't want anyone messing in what he calls his stuff. It's not like I was going to trash it, I was only digging out his dirty clothes like I always do when he comes home, so I can toss 'em in the wash.''

She sighed, and Tucker settled deeper in his chair, the only truly comfortable piece of furniture he owned these days, aside from his bed. ''It's just a stage he's going through, right? The hair—the clothes? The tattoos, only I'm pretty sure those aren't real. It's not like he's trying to hide anything. Tell me I'm just being paranoid, will you do that much?''

''You're being a perfectly normal parent, and Jay's probably a perfectly normal boy on the verge of manhood. And, Tucker, I'm no expert on children. Once, a long time ago, I worked with children, but that was before I disappeared under an avalanche of paperwork. I've noticed, though, that every few years the species seems to reinvent itself. I guess we all do it to one degree or another. Rebel against the previous generation. Otherwise we'd all still be stuck in our great-great-grandparents' world.''

''Did you?'' He couldn't imagine Annie being anything but an obedient little girl.

Or maybe he could. Hadn't he sensed something just underneath that deceptively drab exterior? Something all the more intriguing because it was so unexpected?

That kiss hadn't been a nice-girl reaction. Hell, a few generations ago, it might not even have been legal.

''I cut my hair when I was Jay's age. Really, really short.''

"Did you dye it?"

"You mean like Bernie? Daddy would've been mortified."

"Speaking of Bernie and Harold, what happens when the rebellion arises at both ends and you're caught in the middle?"

She was silent for so long he knew she was genuinely considering his words. "I wonder if Bernie and your Jay would have anything in common. I suspect they might."

"You mean besides Harold?" He chuckled, but to Annie's ears, it had a sad, quietly desperate sound. The sound of a man who needed to be held, with no questions asked.

"Is that a cup of strawberry tea on your bedside table?"

"Half a cup. Cold. How did you know?"

"Lucky guess. What are you reading, poetry? Romance?"

"How To Make a Bundle on a Bear Market."

"You're kidding."

"Tucker, what's really on your mind? If you have any real reason to believe Jay's in trouble, maybe you should talk to his mother. Or someone from his school. Or even Harold. Sometimes grandparents…" She sighed. "But then, I guess Harold has his own problems at the moment. Speaking of which, I might've found a place that's relatively safe, relatively affordable, on a bus route, and best of all, there's no waiting list. I have an appointment to see it in the morning. I plan to take an early lunch."

"Why don't we get together and look it over?"

"Because you've got your hands full, and I don't really need you to make an initial assessment. I'll let you know if I think it's possible, and then you can take a look."

He said something vaguely affirmative, and for a long time neither of them spoke. Annie was thinking, *I'll miss it. The arguments, the drives out to the headless Blue Flamingo. And the other.*

It was "the other" that kept her awake at night, reading dry, plotless nonfiction, trying in vain to get her mind back where it belonged. Back in its customary orderly rut.

"What time will you be home tomorrow?" Tucker asked.

"By six. Possibly earlier."

"Jay and I'll come by and pick you up for pizza and you can fill me in on the apartment. And, Annie—I'd really like you to get to know Jay. What with everything else that's been going on lately, my perspective's about half a bubble off square. Maybe I'm borrowing trouble, but if there's something going on that I'm missing, I need to find out about it. The world's a dangerous place for kids these days."

"I told you, I'm no expert, especially on adolescent boys."

"No, but you're a calm, reasonable, sensible, unflappable woman who can be a hell of a lot more objective than one harried single parent."

"Am I all those things? Mercy, I sound dull as ditch water." The last thing she felt was calm. As for the other—what sensible, reasonable woman got herself engaged to a man who immediately took off for parts unknown, leaving her to keep tabs on his mother while he worked the wanderlust out of his system?

Unflappable? She was beginning to believe she could flap with the best of them, given the opportunity.

"Hey, you still there?"

"I'm trying to decide whether to be insulted or flattered."

"Be flattered. Take it from me, calm and sensible are highly underrated qualities these days." He laughed softly, and the disembodied sound did odd things to her nervous system, things that didn't feel at all calm or sensible. "See you about half past six tomorrow, all right?" And then he said, "Oh, hell, I forgot about what's-his-name. Hey, I wouldn't want to screw up your personal life."

Annie had a feeling she'd done that all by herself, but until she saw Eddie again, she wasn't ready to admit anything. He could show up tonight, tomorrow or a year from now. Reliable, he was not. "Let me think it over. I'll call you after I've seen the apartment, and we'll go from there." She hung up before she could get in any more trouble than she was in already.

It made no sense at all, the effect this man had on her. It was probably only a little-known side effect of lying in bed late at night, talking to a sexy man on the telephone. She'd read somewhere that the imagination was an incredible aphrodisiac.

"Be still, my fevered brain," she muttered as she slid back down in bed and tried to concentrate on bear markets and bull markets and price-earnings ratios.

*   *   *

Annie had just come back from lunch and looking at the apartment when the phone on her desk rang. It was Eddie, calling from Woodbridge, Virginia. He'd stopped off to see an old friend.

"If I decide to stay over tonight, I'll let you know. Would you mind calling Mama and telling her I'll pick her up on the way to your place? I don't want to run up too many charges on my friend's phone bill."

Annie sputtered a little, and Eddie said, "Kiss, kiss," and hung up.

"What about *my* phone bill?" she inquired plaintively of the ceramic lop-eared mouse on her desk. His mother lived in Roanoke, Virginia. Hadn't the man ever heard of reversing the charges?

She knew for a fact that he had, because he'd called her collect several times.

"Balderdash," she muttered, tackling the stack of forms to be filled out before she could go home for the day. Thank goodness they didn't require much concentration, because her brain had developed a mind of its own. With a fiancé, not to mention a future mother-in-law about to descend on her, all she could think of was Tucker Dennis. At least half of what she was thinking was X-rated, and Annie had never even seen an X-rated film. If she had, she might've built up a little more immunity to her own thoughts.

By the time she left for the day, she had firmly made up her mind to stay as far out of Tucker's life as she possibly could. It was the only sensible thing to do. Sooner or later Harold and Bernie would settle down. Not in the apartment she'd looked at that morning, because that was a dump, but somewhere. And once they did, her own life could get back to normal.

Sooner or later Jay would go back to school, and the next time his father saw him, there would be a whole new set of developments to worry about. Maturity evidently occurred in stages, like a jerky elevator on the way to the top floor. She'd skipped a few stops herself, but sooner or later she would arrive at her floor. She and Eddie would be married and she would have her babies and live happily ever after. With no illusions and no romantic dreams to overcome, she would be content, if not wildly happy.

Wild happiness was probably a health risk, anyway. Like too much saturated fat, or a steady diet of chocolate doughnuts. Good while it lasted, but not without costs. There was no room in her life for a man who made her think dangerously physical thoughts. A man who could set her imagination on fire with no more than the deep, rough timbre of his voice and a blaze of those splintery hazel eyes.

Not to mention his kiss. And his touch. And that need she sensed inside him that called out to a part of her buried so deep that she'd never even known of its existence.

Before she left for the day, she called Tucker's office to tell him she wouldn't be available tonight. The phone rang and rang and no one answered, so she tried his home number, but it was busy and stayed busy until she lost patience and dialed Bernie's room at the motel.

No answer. Well, shoot. She'd done her best, that was all anyone could expect of her.

The first thing she saw when she left the administration building was Tucker's silver pickup truck. He was leaning against the hood, one booted foot propped on the hubcap, looking more than ever like something off one of Bernie's posters. It would have helped her wavering resolve if he'd looked more like the responsible, caring son and father she knew him to be, and less like the sexy, dangerous bad-boy her father used to warn her against in veiled, preacherly terms.

Boys are different from girls, daughter.

Well, I know that, Daddy, but you always say we should be kind to those people who're different, because they're God's children, too.

"I tried to call, but you weren't in your office," Tucker said by way of greeting.

"I've been either in meetings or buried under a ton of paperwork, except when I left at eleven."

"Yeah, well—maybe I messed up on the number. It's a little early, but by the time we get to the pizza place, order and get served, it'll be later."

He looked so earnest. As if he had no idea that even his voice could raise goose bumps down her sides.

"I have errands to do. I'd planned to go by a drugstore," she said, determined not to give in too easily.

"Sure, no problem, there's one in the same complex with the pizza place."

Through the driver's side window, she could see a big-knuckled hand beating time on the dashboard. It wasn't like a real date, she rationalized. It was more like a conference. Besides, she really did need to tell him about the apartment.

Excuses, excuses.

After meeting Jay, Annie knew just what Tucker had looked like at that age. Take away the strange hair and the hideous clothes and the sullen expression and you still had the same blunt, angular features. The same thick, level eyebrows. The same mouth, only Jay's was sulky and vulnerable and nowhere near as sensuous as his father's mouth.

Annie had a feeling that one day soon, a lot of fathers would be warning their daughters to stay clear of the Dennis kid. She tried not to stare at his hair. Tucker's was thick, dark brown, laced with silver and about a week overdue for a trim.

Jay's was cut in a scalp lock, or whatever it was called, that had been dyed almost the same shade of orangy-red Bernie used. She wondered if he'd met his new stepgrandmother yet, and if they'd compared notes on color rinses.

Tucker said there was no point in driving two cars through Friday's bumper-to-bumper going-home traffic. This time it was his turn to drive. Jay crawled into the jump seat. So far he hadn't spoken a word, but his eyes, the exact color of seedless green grapes, spoke volumes.

On being introduced, Annie had offered her hand, which had been ignored. Tucker had looked ready to bite off a few heads, but he'd kept his mouth shut. Smart man. He'd clearly learned to pick his battles.

"Heard anything about the cat?" he asked when they stopped at the first light.

"No, and I'm really worried, but after the mouse episode, at least I know he's still in the neighborhood."

They discussed it for a few minutes, ignoring the sullen presence in the back seat.

"Cats," Jay muttered. "They're dumb. There's a guy I know who's into snakes."

Annie glanced at the rearview mirror and saw enough to know he was waiting for some kind of reaction.

She reacted. "Not literally, I hope."

"Huh? What's that mean?"

"The word literally? It implies the exact meaning of a word or a text. Apply it to the exact wording of your statement."

"That this guy is into snakes?" A slow grin spread across his face. "Hey, that's cool. Like he was inside a snake, right? What's that word again? Literally?"

Tucker, looking somewhat dazed, pulled in at a strip mall. "You said you needed a drugstore. Was it a special one, or will this do?"

"A drugstore? Oh. Actually…"

Actually, she'd been going to buy a blusher, an ash-brown rinse and condoms, in case Eddie forgot. Considering how long they'd been separated, something like that might easily slip his mind. At thirty-four, two years younger than she was, he was hardly the most practical man she'd ever met. In college he'd been called the Peter Pan of the Appalachian Trail.

"This is fine," she murmured, and opened the

truck door before Tucker could come around to help her down from the high running board.

"Need some help?"

"What? Oh, no. No, thank you. I'll just be a minute," she said breathlessly.

Remember why you're here, Annie Summers! You're buying condoms for your fiancé's homecoming celebration.

"Tell me again why you use the hair of a deer to make something called a fly to catch fish."

"You're kidding, right?"

Annie wiped the pizza sauce from her fingers and crossed her heart. "I always used catalpa worms. They're free, if you can find a wormy catalpa tree. Not all of them are." She took another big bite of her vegetarian pizza. Tucker was leaning back in the corner of the booth, his gaze going back and forth between them like a spectator at a tennis match. Annie would have given a month's salary to know what he was thinking. Even though she worked at a private school, she didn't really know any children on a personal level. She did know that they were as different from one another as adults were, even though they tried desperately to show their individuality by dressing, speaking and acting alike.

She knew they were terribly fragile, no matter how tough they tried to appear. Jay's crust wasn't nearly as thick as she'd thought at first, it was only skin-deep. Insecurity was her own snap diagnosis. Based on what, she had yet to find out.

Somehow, without knowing how it happened, Annie and Tucker's son had gotten off on the right foot. First she'd taken him off guard by asking him if he used Tropical Treasure, the same color Bernie used, on his hair. Next she'd told him about Zen, and how gorgeous he was, and how wicked, and about the love-hate relationship they shared. It was more of a tolerance-irritation relationship, but still she felt guilty over it, and Annie had always found it hard to deal with feelings of guilt.

Jay responded by telling her more than she really wanted to know about fishing, tracking, what music was "way cool," and some dude named Miller his mom was hanging out with.

Tucker hadn't said a word, except on the few occasions when Jay had said, "Right, Dad?"

Or when Annie had said, "Have you two talked about Harold and Bernie yet?"

Then he'd said, "Yeah, we went over it."

So she'd moved on to a few more topics about which she knew nothing—video games and action movies—and allowed Jay to direct the conversation.

"I'm sorry, " she said at length, "but as enjoyable as this has been, I really do have to get home. I'm expecting house guests," she explained to Jay. "My fiancé has just come back from a long tour of several continents. He called this morning from Virgina, and I'm expecting him late tonight or early tomorrow."

Tucker spoke up then. "We'd better get you home, in that case."

But I don't want to go home, Annie thought. I'm much rather stay here with you, watching your son shed his defensive layers, listening to him brag about his prowess as a fisherman and how cool he is for not caring that his mother is about to marry a man he's never even met.

Jay climbed into the back. Tucker reached out to help Annie into the front seat, and in trying to avoid his touch, she managed to drop both her purse and the bag from the pharmacy.

They both bent down at the same time, Tucker muttering apologies. Annie was busy gathering up her keys and chapstick while Tucker reached under the edge of the truck for the small package that had slithered out of the plastic pharmacy sack.

Oh, God. She would die. She would never be able to look him in the face again after this.

Carefully, as if he hadn't even noticed what it was, Tucker slid the box of condoms into the plastic bag and handed it to her as she scrambled up into the truck.

Annie thought she mumbled her thanks, but she wasn't sure. Her brain was on fire, just like her face.

No one said a word on the drive home. Annie's mind was racing like a mouse on a treadmill. Had he seen it? He couldn't possibly have seen what it was in the time it had taken him to slide it into the bag.

Hair rinse. She'd have been embarrassed enough if he'd seen that, but condoms—!

At least he hadn't said anything. Probably because Jay was there.

And anyway, she was entitled. She was a mature, sensible, engaged woman whose fiancé was coming home after an extended stay abroad. Some women actually carried the things in their purses, like Tums or Excedrin, in case of emergency.

They pulled up in front of her house, and she swung open her door before Tucker could even switch off the engine. "Well. This has been lovely. Thanks for everything," she said with a smile that was as phony as a three-dollar bill. "No, don't bother to get out, the yard light's on a timer. Bye, Jay, and if I don't see you again before you go back to school, remember to try catalpa worms."

She was backing away as she talked. Babbled was more like it.

Because suddenly it was as clear as rainwater. She didn't want them to leave. Ever. She wanted them to come in and let her feed them and make them comfortable and talk to them, and then she wanted to climb the stairs with Tucker's arms around her waist.

She didn't even know Eddie Robertson, much less did she want to marry him and bear his children while he broke still more promises and went traipsing off to heaven knows where, doing heaven knows what, leaving her behind to take care of his babies and his mother.

Eddie's mother called just after the eleven-o'clock weather broadcast. Annie had been on her way upstairs. "I'm worried about my boy. He should've been here by now."

"Oh, dear, I was supposed to call you. I meant to as soon as I got home today, but something came up and I forgot." Annie went on to explain about the call from Woodbridge and listened to Rosa whine about inconsiderate landlords and Medicare forms and a long list of other favorite complaints. Annie had heard them all before.

It was when the older woman said, "In my day, we—" that Annie had had enough.

"Mrs. Robertson, why don't you give me a call when Eddie gets there. Let me know when you plan to leave Roanoke, and I'll have your room all ready and we can talk about it when you get here."

She hung up the phone. "After which," she said gravely, "I'll break every plate in the china cabinet. I'll personally dig up every geranium in the sun parlor and then I'll scream, just to see what it feels like."

What on earth was a woman supposed to do when her life was rushing past at the speed of sound, and she suddenly realized she was on the wrong road?

Nine

$\mathbf{A}$ll the way home from work the next day, Annie added to her mental lists. When things became too chaotic, she had a tendency to do that. To list her newest worries, prioritize them and then proceed to tackle them in an orderly manner.

Only how did a woman prioritize embarrassment? Nebulous longings? Nagging feelings of failure?

Thank goodness there was too much to be done to worry over it. She needed to air Mrs. Robertson's room, dust every piece of furniture, as she had alergies, and chill the supply of imported beer she'd bought for Eddie.

She needed to get out the souvenirs Eddie had sent her from various places and sit them around so that he'd know how much she appreciated his thoughtfulness. If she kept herself busy doing things that had to be done, she might not waste too much time thinking about what she would rather be doing.

Such as telling her guests to make themselves at home, walking out the door, finding Tucker, sending Jay back to his mother and then making wild, passionate love to the man for days, or hours, or minutes—or however long wild, passionate love could last. In her experience it lasted minutes and wasn't particularly wild.

And she would like to do it all without speaking a single word.

So much for reasonable.

Eddie had spent the night and another day in Woodbridge before picking up his mother. The two of them would be arriving about eight, barring heavy traffic.

She tried not to think of Eddie's driving. He treated the highway as if it were his own personal property, racing along at eighty miles an hour with the windows open to feel the wind in his face; slowing down suddenly to admire a patch of wildflowers or a deer grazing on the right-of-way.

Once she'd considered whimsy in a man Eddie's age rather endearing.

Which probably said more about her than about Eddie.

They got in shortly before ten. Eddie had stopped off twice to drop in on old friends along the way, and Rosa Robertson was fit to be tied. They'd dined with a Taiwanese couple in Danville, as they'd been running so late. "I knew you'd understand, luv. Mama was hungry."

"I couldn't eat a bite of that mess they put on the table. Annie, do you have any Pepto-Bismol?"

"In the bathroom closet, second shelf, right hand side." As soon as she left, Annie turned to her fiancé. "Of course I'd have understood, if you'd bothered to call and tell me."

"Uh-oh. I goofed, didn't I? But wait'll you see what I brought you, luv." He said it that way. Not love, but luv.

From there, things went downhill. Mrs. R. couldn't sleep on feather pillows, Annie should have remembered. Her room was too cold; quilts were too heavy, she would much prefer a duvet. And she wanted a thermos of cool, not cold, water beside her bed in case she needed to take a pill in the night when her sinuses started acting up, as they always did when she had to sleep in an unaired room.

"Mrs. Robertson, the room was aired. That's why it's still chilly, because I opened the windows as soon as I got home from work."

"Annie, where's this week's TV schedule? There's a special on the Travel Channel tonight that I've been dying to see—I'm in it, unless I got edited out. There was this fabulous shot of me crossing a raging river with Donna and Steff and some of the trekkers, and…"

Annie tuned out. It was already nearing midnight. So much for condoms. She'd known even when she'd bought them that she didn't want to use them. Not with Eddie, who had proposed for reasons that were even more obscure than her own reason for accepting.

Just how sacred was a promise? Was it more honorable to uphold a promise given in haste, or to admit that she'd changed her mind and beg forgiveness? She might feel responsible for him, but she could never love him. Not with the same breathless, compelling, heart-stopping intensity that came over her whenever she even thought about Tucker Dennis.

They made it through the weekend without actually coming to blows, although several times Annie had to pull on a sweater and walk around the block a few times. It helped that she didn't see all that much of Eddie, who had gone to high school at Reynolds, and spent most of the time looking up old classmates.

"I smell cat. Do you have a cat around here, Annie?"

So Annie explained about Bernie and Zen, and that Bernie was married now and the cat was temporarily lost. "He's around the neighborhood somewhere, I'm pretty sure. He leaves calling cards."

"Yes, well, you know how I am about cats. At least I had the courtesy to put Bootsie in a kennel. I left one of my slippers with him so he wouldn't get lonesome."

Against all reason, Annie began to long for Bernie and her boom box and her MTV and her *Penthouse* and *Playgirl* magazines hastily slipped behind pillows when Annie walked in unexpectedly.

Once when she'd come back for a book she'd forgotten and found Bernie still in her robe and hair rollers, having a second cup of coffee, Bernie had automatically slid a magazine under the chair cushion, then yanked it out again. It turned out to be a copy of *Modern Maturity*. They'd both had a good laugh.

Life was dull. Mrs. R. was dull, Annie was dull, they were all dull. Even Peter Pan grew boring after a while. Bernie might be exasperating, but no one could ever accuse her of being dull. When Tucker called during *60 Minutes* on Sunday night to say he'd located a sublease and had the key, and would Annie like to take a look at it, she jumped at the chance to escape.

"I've got to go out for a little while," she announced, feeling as if someone had opened the door and let in a gust of fresh air.

"That's all right, dear. Would you mind turning up the heat a smidge before you go? You always keep it so cold in here."

Eddie smiled that boyish, beguiling smile of his— a smile that was as shallow as his promises—and said, "Drive carefully, luv. I'll never get used to all the crazy drivers you have here in the States these days."

Here in the States? Eddie had started crossing his sevens after his very first trip abroad so that no one would ever mistake him for a provincial.

Annie wanted to ask what was so wrong with being a provincial. She wanted to say, you're the biggest hazard on the highway, but didn't, because he wouldn't understand, and she had neither the energy nor the interest to explain.

"You look bushed," Tucker said when he came by to pick her up. She'd waited for him on the front porch, too tired to get into introductions and explanations.

"Thanks," she said dryly. "So do you."

"Too much boyfriend?"

"Too much mother-in-law. Too much travelogue. Too much heat. To much..." And then she laughed. "Listen to me, I'm beginning to sound just like Mrs. R. Everything's too much or too little, too hot or too cold, too salty, and for heaven's sake, don't I know a body can't cook greens without fatback?"

Annie laughed, bit her lip, and somehow or another found herself being wrapped in Tucker's arms. For reasons she didn't even want to think about, her eyes began to water.

"I'm not crying, honestly. I think I must have caught Rosa's allergy. Oh, God, Tucker, I can't bear to spend the rest of my life like this."

"Like this?" His arms tightened around her, and suddenly she became aware of the crisp scent of leather and aftershave. Of cold, refreshing, damp air. Of a hard male body moving, growing harder, changing shape.

"We'd better get going," he said gruffly, and handed her up into the high four-by-four.

They drove in silence, which allowed Annie time to regain her composure. She did it by blocking out everything but the task at hand. Finding a suitable place for Harold and Bernie, so everyone could settle down and get on with their lives.

The sublease was in the West End area, a restored post-Victorian, physically similar to Annie's own house, but in far better condition. As soon as Tucker switched off the lights and ignition, Annie opened her door. She didn't need to be helped, didn't want to be touched. Didn't want it because she craved it entirely too much.

"There are five apartments, two on the first floor, two on the second and one on the third."

Annie wasn't interested in the third floor. They'd already plowed that field, as her father would've said. He'd been the first in a long line of corn, cotton and soybean farmers to attend college, but he'd never outgrown his country roots.

"Bernie's arthritis, remember? One flight of stairs she can deal with, but any more than that gives her trouble."

She turned to look at him just as they reached the bottom of a flight of wide wooden steps to the house. Her toe bumped against the riser and she flung out her arms for balance.

"Whoa, watch it," Tucker muttered and before she could recover he was holding her again.

It was like coming home. Standing there, his arms around her waist, her hands clutching his shoulders, her face buried in the cool surface of his leather jacket.

Someone drove by on the hilly, curving boulevard and let loose a long, low whistle. Annie jumped guiltily. Tucker's arms tightened. "We'd better go inside," he said. "I wouldn't want to ruin your reputation, you being an assistant principal and all."

Once inside, Tucker led her toward the stairs, his arm still around her waist as if he'd forgotten to remove it. "Nice wainscotting. Shame to carpet these quarter-cut oak floors. The place is available monthly through August. Naturally, there are a few restrictions, but the rent's pretty reasonable.''

"Tucker, don't change the subject. Bernie's arthritis? We've been over this before.'' But with his arms around her, the crisp, clean scent of him so near, her voice carried little conviction. "I don't suppose this place runs to an elevator, does it?''

"Probably not. The ad said it was a walk-up. I was just so damned glad to get a lead, I didn't think about the drawbacks. We might as well take a look, though, as long as we're here.''

The odor of something being fried drifted up the stairs along with them. On the second floor someone was playing a radio softly. Schubert. She could imagine the disruptive effect Bernie would have on the other residents.

Halfway to the top, the narrow stairway took a right angle turn. "Watch your head,'' Tucker warned a split second too late.

Annie was just tall enough so that the top of her head caught a jutting dip in the ceiling, one of several that had been designed to accommodate the intricacies of the roof.

"Oh, dammit to hell,'' she muttered, slapping a hand to her forehead. Tucker stared at her as if a frog had jumped out of her mouth.

The tears that sprang to her eyes were more a result of utter discouragement than pain. It was as if they welled up from a hollow place deep in her soul that was growing faster than she could plaster it over.

"Hey, are you all right?'' he asked softly, examining her forehead for damage. Finding none, he gazed into her eyes, looking puzzled. "I've never heard you talk like that before."

"There's nothing wrong with my vocabulary," she informed him, climbing the remaining few steps. "As a rule I use more discretion, but there comes a time when crying 'Mercy, mercy, mercy,' just doesn't get the job done."

She stepped out into the plainly furnished apartment and pretended an interest, even thought they both knew it was out of the question. He was hovering over her, waiting to see if she was going to fall apart.

"You're sure there's not anything available on the first floor?"

"'Fraid not."

She crossed her arms defensively, as if that alone could shield her from his magnetism and her own weakness. "Then this is an utter waste of time."

"Think so? What if I told you I knew all along it was out of the question, that I just wanted to get you away, and this was the only excuse I could come up with?"

"Away from what?"

"What do you think? Away from what's-his-name."

"But why?" She felt breathless, possibly because her heart seemed to have become lodged somewhere in the vicinity of her larynx. "Because you need to talk to me? Is it something to do with Bernie and Harold?"

"Try again."

"Is it Jay? Are you having problems?"

He was so close she could feel the warmth of his breath in the chilly attic. "No more than usual. Something's bugging him, but I guess it'll come out in due time."

"Then what?" she wailed. In the light of the single table lamp Tucker had switched on when they'd reached the top of the stairs, his features looked more angular than ever, his eyes nearly black.

"Look, there's no fancy way to say this, so don't fly off the handle, okay?"

"Tucker, just say it. I've never flown off a handle in my life, but I will if you don't tell me what this is all about."

"Yeah, well—that's the problem. I'm not really sure. The thing is, I'm used to playing my cards pretty close to my vest, but for some reason I keep wanting to run things by you to get your take."

Could he possibly be jealous because of the way she and Jay had hit it off? "Look, your son and I found a few areas of common ground, that's all. Sometimes it's easier to talk to a stranger because they're not a part of the problem."

"This is not about Jay. Oh, a part of it, maybe, but the thing is, I keep finding myself wanting to share things with you—things I read in the paper or hear on the news. I've never felt like that before. I sure as hell didn't with my ex-wife. It's flat-out spooky."

"It's not at all spooky. You're divorced. Your son's usually away at school. Your father's recently remarried. It's only natural for you to feel lonely now and then."

He made a sound that defied interpretation. Clasping the back of his neck with one hand, he turned away and scowled at the toe of his shoe. He wasn't wearing boots tonight. He wasn't wearing jeans or khakis. When he'd first shown up, she'd been so glad to see him she hadn't even noticed what he was wearing. Now she did. Nice brown casual shoes that looked expensive. Dark slacks, a light-blue dress shirt, no tie and his leather jacket.

He looked handsome, mature and dangerously sexy.

He smelled even better. Like wood smoke, leather and evergreens.

"That's a bunch of bull," he said, his voice low and raspy.

"What's a bunch of bull?"

"That I'm lonely. Hell, in the first place I don't have time to be lonely."

"Being lonely doesn't require a whole lot of time."

He looked at her as if trying to read beyond her words. It was one of those electric moments she had read about, but never—at least until recently—experienced. Then, in a gesture that managed to combine bafflement, exasperation and helplessness, he flung out his arms. "Look, I know it doesn't make sense, but the thing is, I can't get it off my mind. Ever since I kissed you—ever since I saw those damned condoms you bought—all I can think of is what it would be like to make love to you. To have sex with you. What I'm trying to say is—"

"I *know* what you're trying to say, Tucker, you don't have to draw a diagram." She sucked in a lungful of air and forgot to breathe out. Her skin was burning. "It's called lust. It's a perfectly normal reaction among men and woman, only in our case it doesn't even make sense."

"Tell me about it," he said bitterly. "Until about a week ago, we'd never spoken a civil word to each other."

"*One* of us had never spoken a civil word. I don't remember calling you names, or—"

"Calling a guy a Neanderthal with a steroid-inflated ego, that's considered polite in your circles?"

"Yes, well…occasionally I might slip up. I was under a lot of stress at the time."

"Are you saying I wasn't?"

"Tucker, none of that matters, the thing is—well, the thing is—"

"Right. The thing is, you've got a fiancé and a box of supplies waiting at home—unless you've already used them all. I've got a debt load that would break a mule, and an ex-wife who pretty well immunized me from this kind of thing."

Ignoring the remark about supplies, Annie picked up the litany. "Besides which, I'm not the type of woman you'd ever look twice at in the normal course of events." She waited desperately for him to deny it.

He didn't. "Right. If I ever had a type, you're not it, and I'm sure as hell not yours."

"I never actually said that."

"Not in so many words—you're too polite. That's one more way we're different. I'm a believer in plain speaking, you hide behind a lot of fancy words."

"I don't hide behind—"

"You're a coward, Annie Summers. You're doing your level best right now to duck out on the truth."

There they stood, in an impersonal apartment, separated by a few feet of commercial-grade carpet and a lifetime of conditioning. And all Annie could think of was that there had to be a bedroom in this place, and if the world ended tomorrow, she'd kick herself all the way to kingdom come for not grabbing what he was offering.

"Are you saying you want to sleep with me?" Her voice sounded as if it came from one of those tinny, old-fashioned phonographs, the kind with a horn.

"So bad I'm damn near crippled. Right now I can't think of anything else. How's that for romantic?"

"I don't expect you to be romantic."

"No? Then would you let me take you to bed, Annie?"

The house could've been shaken on its foundation by an earthquake. A war could've broken out on the floors below, and neither of them would've noticed. "Yes, please," she whispered.

For an instant he looked stunned. And then his eyes narrowed so that all she could see was twin slits of obsidian. "I can't make you any offers."

"I haven't asked for anything."

"What about what's-his-name?"

She held up her left hand. No ring. "We haven't got round to breaking things off formally, but we both know it's not going to work."

"Maybe we should wait till it's official?" His face

was flushed. Every muscle in his large body was tensed.

"If we wait, it's not going to happen. I know me. Right now, I want you to make love to me more than I want to draw my next breath, but if I wait—if I have time to think about it—"

"You'll back off."

She nodded. "Blame it on a lifetime of conditioning. Duty, responsibility, nice girls don't—that sort of thing."

"But you want to?"

It was as if they were standing on separate ice floes that were rapidly drifting apart. One of them had to jump, and jump fast.

Annie jumped. Wordlessly she nodded, and that was all it took. His arms went around her in a fierce embrace. Quickly his face went out of focus as he lowered his mouth to hers.

There was a bedroom. There was a bed. There was a spread on the bed, but no sheets. The room was musty, as if it hadn't been used in a long time. Tucker shed his coat and opened a window to let in the damp, cool spring air. Then he turned and looked at her for several long moments.

"I can't believe I didn't see how beautiful you were that first day. I guess I was too busy trying to get past your defenses."

Annie didn't even pretend not to watch him as he unbuttoned his shirt and shrugged it off his shoulders. "I don't have any defenses," she declared. He wasn't wearing an undershirt. There was a neat pattern of hair that streaked down his flat diaphragm from his pectorals to disappear under his belt.

She swallowed hard.

His eyes never left her as his hands moved to the plain brass buckle. He made short work of it, then found the tab of his zipper. The evidence of his arousal was so powerful she caught her breath.

Oh, my mercy. What if she couldn't—what if he didn't—"Tucker, I don't have, um—birth control."

"I do." His voice was as dark as his eyes, hard, flat and glittering.

She thought, he looks like a stranger.

And then she thought, he *is* a stranger.

Totally naked, he stood there and allowed her to look her fill. It occurred to the small portion of her brain that hadn't yet shut down that it took a man secure in his own masculinity to allow a fully clothed woman to stare at him in this condition.

He was large. She wondered if he was offering her a chance to back out. Somehow, she was certain that if she wanted out, he wouldn't try to keep her there.

"Seen enough? Your turn, then," he said.

She crossed her arms over her chest and felt like an absolute idiot. An experienced thirty-six-year-old woman, and she was reacting like a trembling virgin.

He began to undress her, gently uncrossing her arms to get to the buttons on her cardigan. Tossing it onto a chair, he sat on the edge of the bed and pulled her toward him, her head on his shoulder, so that he could get at the buttons on the back of her plain beige silk blouse.

She was wearing a slip. She always wore a slip.

He looked frustrated for half a moment, then reached for the waistband of her skirt. "Ladies wear too da— too many clothes," he said, and she laughed, although it sounded more like a sob, at the thought that for the occasion, he was trying hard not to swear. A real gentleman. Her father would've approved of him.

Oh, God, Annie, this is no time to be thinking about your father, not when you're about to commit a sin of the flesh.

He took his time, his callused hands, hard and warm, lingering on her shoulders, slowly sliding the straps of her plain white bra down and then cupping her breasts before moving on to her panty hose.

By then she was lying down on the hard mattress, twisting and biting her lip. Every part of her body, right down to her toes, was on fire. She knew what sex was all about. She had read the books, done the deed several times and studied the diagrams in her gynecologists's office.

Nothing had prepared her for this. For Tucker.

He didn't try to rush her, even though he was trembling with his own urgent need. Instead, he led her oh, so slowly, ever so tenderly, to the point where she was out of her mind.

First with his hands and then his mouth, he sent her splintering into a million pieces without ever allowing her to touch him.

And she wanted to. She tried, but each time, he covered her hands with his and moved them to his lips. "Annie, don't. Not yet. Short fuse—been a long time, too long. I'll embarrass us both. Wait."

Each word emerged as a separate gasp. She

vaguely understood, but this was so far from anything she had ever experienced before that she might as well be on a different planet, making love with an alien species.

Finally he moved over her, having driven her to the brink of madness again and again, only to revive her with a touch, a kiss. She gazed up into the strained face of a stranger who was as familiar to her as her own right hand. A stranger she had known forever in ways she didn't even try to comprehend.

This was Tucker. Irascible, lovable, tough, wonderfully caring Tucker. Somehow, in the space of eternity, plus two short weeks, had she fallen in love.

Gently at first, he entered her. Tremors shook his powerful, braced arms as he surged inside her and began to move. His eyes were closed. Hers remained open, marveling at what was happening to her, until the very last moment. Until the world disappeared once more in an explosion of shattering rainbows and sensory fireworks.

Tucker groaned. "Annie, Annie, I can't—"

He thrust once more, shuddered, and then they both collapsed.

A cool wind blew over their damp bodies. Gradually Annie came to her senses enough to realize that even in a moment of extreme stress, he had shifted so as to relieve her of his weight.

She wanted it back. The weight. The bliss. Whatever it was—she knew the clinical term, but it didn't come close to describing what had just happened to her.

Bliss did. And she wanted it back.

"Tucker, are you awake?" she murmured, wondering how she could get through the rest of her life knowing such ecstasy existed and being deprived of it.

"Not sleeping, only dead."

"Oh."

That settled that, then. Sex was bound to take a lot out of a man. From some more than others, she thought, and then tried not to compare, because she'd always been taught that comparisons were odious.

She was hugging his arm, needing to hold on to him in some way, for as long as she could. They were both damp and slick and probably generating steam in the cool room.

"Tucker?"

He snored softly. Annie let him sleep while she struggled to arrange her thoughts in some kind of order. She had a feeling none of her neat, organized systems for managing her life were going to work after this.

Now what, Annie? No promises, no commitments, remember?

The house was dark when she got home. The yard light was on, but Eddie had forgotten to leave a light on inside. But then, she'd have been more surprised if he had. In so many ways he was as thoughtless as a child.

"I'll see you inside, all right?"

"No, don't. Everyone's asleep and—Tucker, what about Jay? Won't he worry if you stay out too late?"

"Harold and Bernie dropped by earlier. They'll stay until I get back."

They were speaking in hushed tones, as if afraid of being overheard by her sleeping fiancé and his mother inside the dark old Victorian house.

"You didn't tell me they were there. Tucker, what—"

"Shhh. We'll talk tomorrow. Everything's under control, all right?"

"Nothing's under control and you know it. If something's come up, you should've told me—"

He cut off her arguments in the most effective way possible. Long moments later, when they came up for air, he whispered, "Tomorrow, all right? Things get all skewed out of shape this time of night." He saw her to the door and then left without looking back.

The living room was a mess. Annie switched on a table lamp, turned off the TV, collected two plates, a cup and saucer, a wineglass and a napkin full of crumbs.

Things were skewed out of shape, all right, she thought as she tiptoed up the stairs to her bedroom. Case in point, her own neat, orderly life.

Ten

Making coffee for Eddie, cocoa for Rosa and tea for herself the next morning, Annie wondered if last night had been only a wild dream. Would a wild dream have caused tenderness in certain parts of her body? Caused the slip she'd put on the right way to be inside out when she'd removed it before falling into her bed?

She couldn't suppress the mild revulsion she felt when Eddie sauntered into the kitchen and greeted her with a glancing kiss on the cheek. "Annie, you don't mind if I make another long-distance call on your phone, do you?"

Another one? "Don't you have a cell phone?"

"Gad, luv, you know me and technology."

"They're not all that expensive. Most people have

them these days.'' Annie didn't, but then she'd always valued her privacy. She didn't want to make herself too available.

"I'll look into it," he promised, dipping a wet finger into the sugar bowl and sucking it.

The perennial Peter Pan. Annie happened to know he had a perfectly good college degree, never mind that his major had been something called The Creative Traditions of Folk Culture. For all his whimsical charm, he was not an uneducated man.

"Just one quick call, luv, that's all. I'll pay you back."

She hated it when he wheedled. He was an expert wheedler, and she always ended up feeling like a stern disciplinarian. Like her own father, in fact.

"Eddie, you don't have to pay me back. Make all the calls you want. If you need more privacy, you can use the upstairs extension."

"Just a quick one, I promise, luv." He loped up the stairs, graceful as a young buck in his soft moccasins. Annie sighed and turned back to the stove.

Rosa waited for her cocoa to be poured, tasted it and wrinkled her nose. "Bitter. And eggs don't taste the way they used to, either. Is that real bacon or that fake stuff they make out of turkey parts?"

Wordlessly Annie slid the sugar bowl across the table.

"Eddie's going to drive me home today. Bootsie hates being boarded. He won't eat a bite if I'm not there to feed him, so I promised him I wouldn't be gone long."

As it hadn't seemed polite to ask how long they

planned to stay, Annie hadn't. Relief flooded her, followed by guilt. She opened a jar of ginger marmalade she'd gotten for Christmas and said, "You might like this—it came from Scotland."

"Ginger? Spices don't sit well on my delicate stomach. Eddie said he'd be coming right back so you two can work out your plans, but don't forget, my lease is coming up for renewal. There's no point in having to pay out anymore, now that your cousin's moved out."

Annie closed her eyes and stood stock-still for a moment. Shouting "Mercy, mercy, mercy!" wouldn't do it. She thought of all the ugly words that preacher's children weren't supposed to know, but invariably did, burned her hand on the omelet pan heating on the stove, then focused her mind on cooking eggs, broiling turkey bacon and making whole wheat toast.

It occurred to her that Eddie seemed no more eager to get on with making plans for the future than she was, but that might be only wishful thinking on her part.

"You forgot I only eat white bread. The brown kind gets under my teeth."

"It's whole wheat or nothing, I'm afraid."

Rosa ate three slices, slathered with butter and the ginger marmalade. To take away the grainy taste, or so she said. By the time Eddie finished with his one brief call, his breakfast was cold. Annie toyed with the notion of scraping it into a plate for the cat, and then remembered that he was still missing. One more weight on her conscience.

"I'll never get used to the water here," Rosa complained. "That's why I asked for cocoa, the tea and coffee are so awful in North Carolina. In Roanoke we have—"

"I'm afraid I'm going to have to rush off," Annie broke in to say. "I'm already an hour late for work."

What if she simply walked out the door and never looked back? Was there still a French Foreign Legion? Did it admit women?

She called the school secretary and said she'd be in as soon as she could make it, and was told not to hurry. "Old Willy's taken one of his spells." Old Willy was Mr. William MacWilliams, the principal. "From the way he's sitting, sort of sidesaddle if you know what I mean, I think his you-know-what must be acting up again."

Annie didn't-know-what. She didn't *want* to know what. From the sound of the clanking pipes, Eddie had borrowed her shower. And probably her fragrance-free soap and her olive oil shampoo and anything else that struck his fancy.

And she didn't begrudge him a bit of it, she really didn't, only it would've been nice if he'd bothered to ask.

She told Mrs. R. that as much as she hated to seem ungracious, she simply had to leave for work, and that it had been lovely having her.

"It's just a shame you had to go out last night. You and Eddie could've had everything all settled by now."

"I know, I'm sorry, too." *Please, God, let me get by with that one small lie, because if You don't, I'm afraid I might do something truly dramatic.*

"Don't you worry, though, he'll probably be back by the time you get home from school. Donna's gone to visit her sister in Newport News."

Donna who? Donna what? Where had she heard that name before?

She didn't want to know. With any luck at all, Eddie would think of at least a dozen more people he needed to visit, and she could put off the unpleasant task of breaking her farce of an engagement a little longer.

Surely it wouldn't come as any great surprise. She'd stopped wearing her ring months ago when she'd developed an itchy rash on the fingers of her left hand and had never gotten back into the habit of wearing it. If Eddie had even noticed, he hadn't bothered to comment. He'd never been overly romantic. Sweet, whimsical, even childlike in some ways, but romantic?

Never. He'd kissed her all of three times this trip. This morning on the cheek, once on the nose when she'd snapped a sharp retort at something he'd said and once on the lips when he'd first arrived. She'd had to keep herself from wiping it off. If she'd been in any doubt as to the state of her heart, that had settled it.

Tucker spent the morning arguing with the perk tester from the health department, who didn't want to certify the last three lots for more than a two-bedroom house, regardless of the fact that each lot was better than seven acres. The problem, Tucker was fairly sure, was that the man had recently certified a block of fifty-foot lots in a development less than a mile south, and now seven out of ten of those lots were having serious septic tank troubles. The man's career was on the line.

Calling on his rapidly diminishing supply of tact, Tucker managed to postpone the final decision. Maybe by the time the last stretch of road was finished and the lots were officially on sale, a miracle would happen. The field inspector would decide to retire. The city would extend septic lines a couple of miles farther out.

"Right. Meanwhile, watch out for low-flying hogs," he muttered.

At least he'd found a temporary solution to one of his problems. Harold had brought Jay out to fish the pond for a few hours early that morning, and then he and Bernie had taken him to the mall.

Twenty minutes ago they'd arrived back at the site with lunch. Harold and Bernie took theirs down to the pond, leaving Tucker and Jay at the field office to chow down on chili dogs and peach milkshakes. "Man, can Grandma evermore play computer games!"

"Grandma?"

Jay shrugged his broad, bony shoulders. "She said I could call her Bernie, but Harold said I should call her Grandma. He said it would make her feel more like one of the family."

"Harold's one of the family. You don't call him Grandpa."

"Yeah, well—he knows he's family. I don't have to keep reminding him."

They'd been through the generational name thing before, the first time Jay had called him Tucker. "All the guys at school call their old man by his first name," he'd boasted. "It's way cool, man. Like friends or something."

"I'm your friend. I'm also your father. Dad will do. Or Pop, or Father if you want to be formal." That had settled the matter for the time being, but something was still eating at the boy. Tucker didn't know how to approach it, as friend or father. He had only a few more days to work things out before Jay had to leave for school.

Unless school itself was the problem. They'd gone a few rounds about that, too. About his grades and the report from his counselor. Jay had promised to try harder, and Tucker had left it at that. Being fourteen was tough enough, any way you looked at it.

It had to be especially tough when your family splintered around you; when the house you'd grown up in was no longer home, and when the people who were supposed to be there for you, weren't.

If having a new grandma helped, then Tucker would do what he could to see that things worked out. The first thing he had to do, though, was pry that pair loose from the headless Blue Flamingo.

Which led directly to the subject he'd been trying all morning to avoid.

What the devil had be been thinking last night, to pull a stunt like that? A one-night stand with a lady of the evening was one thing, but Annie was off-limits. There was no future in it. Given the connection, there was also no way he could avoid seeing her unless one or the other of them moved out of town.

On the other hand, she was a sensible woman. She knew the score. What if he offered to make a few repairs on her house and agreed to cut her cousin some slack? All he needed in return was someone to share his bed occasionally. Someone to laugh at his jokes and hash over the editorial pages with him—someone to let him blow off steam when he needed a sounding board, and stay the hell out of his personal life.

Right. What woman could turn down an offer like that? "You're a real prince, Dennis."

No wonder he hadn't been able to hold on to a wife. No wonder he was having trouble communicating with his son. No wonder—

Before he could beat up on himself any further, Harold and Bernie wandered back up the hill to collect Jay, who had eaten everything in sight, including the stash of junk food Tucker kept on hand for emergencies.

They were holding hands. Harold was wearing his poker face, which always meant he was up to something. "Y'know, Bernie and I were thinking. Why don't we have us a family cookout, sort of celebrate Jay's spring break? We can stop by the market on the way home. Jay, you said you needed a few things. Your dad can pick up Annie on the way home, and by that time I'll have the grill all fired up."

Talk about your worst nightmares. Tucker opened his mouth to object, then shut it again. "What about it, son?"

Jay was messing with the office computer. He shrugged. "Yeah, I guess."

"Don't do us any favors," Bernie snapped. "There's a 'Return to Woodstock' special on tonight and I aim to watch it, so don't look for me to be doing any entertaining."

Jay twisted his head around, throwing his Adam's apple into prominence. "Was Jimmy Hendrix there?"

"Where, Woodstock? You bet your bony butt he was. They all were, all the great ones."

"Cool."

"Looks like we got us a deal then," Harold said smugly. "Bernie and I'll spring for burgers and buns. I'll do the grilling, and, Tuck, you and Annie stop and get ice cream."

"Does Annie know about this?"

"Not yet," Bernie told him. Her stop-sign-red lipstick was smeared. "She'll go for it, though. She's had that pair of leeches all weekend, she'd be needing a break."

After they'd gone, Tucker jerked open a desk drawer with twice the force necessary and then had to rearrange the contents. He was ticked. Royally ticked off. He'd had a plan, dammit—at least he'd been working on one, and now he was going to have to socialize with the woman in front of his family and pretend nothing had happened last night. He wasn't that great an actor.

Second-cousins-in-law. Yeah, right. So why was his groin hardening, if that's all they were? Why was he already thinking of ways to get her away from the others?

He told himself he only wanted to get her alone so they could talk it out, try and make sense of this craziness between them and lay out a few ground rules for the occasional family get-togethers that were bound to take place over the years.

When no easy answers came to mind, Tucker shut the door behind him and stalked off up the hill to what had become his favorite place on the entire tract.

So what if the contractor still hadn't finished clearing the roads? So what if the entire twenty-odd acres wouldn't perk? That didn't stop the wind from blowing through the red oaks, tulip poplars and sycamores. It didn't keep the wild cherries from budding, or the birds from scouting out nesting sites. It didn't keep him from dropping down onto a fallen log to gaze morosely down on the pond through the woods.

As long as there were places like this where he could be alone, he might stand a chance of getting his head straight. Annie had said she listed her worries according to priority. Her method made sense. First do the things that could be done quickest, thus easing the pressure by shortening the length of the list.

Tucker had his own list, only he hadn't even made an effort to arrange things in any order. The property. Finding a decent house to live in instead of the dump he was renting. Getting his eyes examined. It had been three years. Getting Harold settled.

There was no telling how that situation would turn out. He'd about given up on trying to meddle. In the end it was Harold's call.

Then there was Jay. The boy was changing so fast

it was hard to know what was going on inside his head. Almost as hard as keeping him in shoes. Tucker had an idea Jay's current problem had something to do with Shelly and this new guy she was seeing, but then, Shelly had been seeing other men since before their own marriage ended. Tucker hadn't known about it at the time. He was pretty sure Jay had never had a clue.

But something was sure as hell bugging the kid, causing the shutters to come down over those clear green eyes whenever Tucker probed too deeply about his future plans. He was going to have to pry hard enough to get to the root of the problem, but not hard enough to scare him into closing up. It was a tall order for a guy whose people skills were notoriously low.

Oh, yeah, he had a long list of worries to keep him lying awake into the night. And right up there at the top was Annie Summers. What the devil was he going to do about Annie?

He knew what he *wanted* to do.

And it scared the hell out of him.

Eleven

For the first time in more years than she could remember, Annie pleaded a headache and left work
early, with a long list of calls waiting to be returned
and a stack of forms still to be dealt with. She really
did have a headache, but normally she would simply
have massaged a few pressure points and ignored it.

"It has to be these damned glasses," she muttered
on the way to her car, and then realized what she'd
said and grimaced.

And then she deliberately said it again. She might
have led a relatively sheltered life as a child, but she
was thirty-six years old, for heaven's sake. Life was
no longer *A Child's Garden of Verses.* One couldn't
even keep up with the news these days without being
offended.

For years she had done her best to uphold the standards that had been drilled into her by her parents. *That Annie Summers is a credit to her raising.*

But that was then and this was now. And besides, her head hurt.

So she said it again. "Damn." But even angry, aching and frustrated, she couldn't bring herself to embellish it any further.

While she checked her tires to be sure they were all still inflated and glanced into the back seat to be sure no one was waiting to attack her, her mind automatically sifted through the list of matters waiting to be dealt with at home.

Eddie. That had to come first. Four years ago in a weak moment she had gotten herself engaged to a man who'd admitted that he was fascinated by her calm, sensible approach to life. Flattered, she had foolishly read into it something that wasn't there. Opposites attract, he'd said, and for a while she'd actually believed him. His wanderlust as opposed to her utter lack of it. His whimsy as opposed to her practicality.

Well, now she was about to get herself unengaged. It would be embarrassing, but embarrassment rarely proved fatal.

When, she wondered as she backed out of her parking slot, had her legendary common sense deserted her? Last night, when she'd slept with a man who was little more than a stranger? Something she had no intention of ever doing again?

But then, that put it squarely in the category of a

one-night stand. Fleetingly she wondered if there was such a thing as a two-night stand.

A five-night stand?

A ten-year stand?

Did the degree of shame decrease with the length of the involvement?

Pulling up at a stoplight, she tried to remember the name of the movie in which Peter Somebody-or-other had leaned out a window and declared to the world that he was mad as hell and wasn't going to take it any longer.

It might work for Peter; it probably wouldn't for Annie. At this point she had no clear thought of what she was going to do next. Sleep, perhaps. Sleep until her life began to make sense again.

Waiting for the light to turn green, she decided that first she would clean and air out the two guest rooms, wash and put away the good china. That done, she would make herself a pot of tea and sit in the front parlor, enjoying a few moments of lovely silence.

"While you're at it, picture yourself growing old all alone with your geraniums and a houseful of evil-tempered cats," she said, cautiously creeping forward in the line of traffic. "If the roof leaks you can simply close off the third floor. And then the second floor. By the time it drips through to the first floor, you'll be too old and dotty to worry about it."

Or maybe, she mused as she slowed to make the turn into her driveway, she would dye her hair orange and find herself a sweet old widower, someone like Harold Dennis, who knew how to fix things like leaky roofs and leaky valves. She'd have to give Bernie credit for her taste in men, if nothing else.

With a heavy sigh she opened her car door, and there he was, standing astride that big old bike of his, looking mean and miserable and determined.

"Annie? I called the school. They said you'd left."

"Oh, for heaven's sake, you scared the wits out of me!"

"We need to talk. They're all coming over to my place pretty soon. I'm supposed to bring you and the ice cream, but I thought we'd better get together first and settle on what we're going to tell them."

"If I'm supposed to connect the dots and make sense of all that, you'll have to start over. Tell whom about what?"

"Our folks, that's whom. Harold, Bernie and Jay. About—well, hell, you know what I mean."

"You think I'm going to tell anyone that we *slept together?*"

"Is that what you call it?"

"Yes, it is. And I'd prefer you to call it that, too, if you don't mind. Better yet, don't call it anything. I intend to forget the whole tawdry affair. It never happened."

"The hell it didn't!"

"Tucker, if you don't mind, I've had a stressful day. My plans for the evening do not include— What did you say they were doing?"

"Who, Harold, Bernie and Jay? They're headed over to my place to fire up the grill. We're having a family cookout."

"Oh, no. Count me out."

"What's the matter, second-cousin-in-law, you don't like my family?"

They were standing in what her father had called the porte cochere. Annie called it what it was, a covered driveway. From a glaringly blue sky, the sun glinted off the black helmet Tucker had just removed. Pain throbbed behind her eyes, at her temples, at the back of her head. "One hour," she whispered. "Was that too much to ask? One hour when I didn't have to smile, or be polite, or be a credit to anyone?"

"You've lost me."

"If that's an offer, I accept." She was tempted to tell him to go to the devil. The trouble was, she was even more tempted to invite him inside, into her bed, into her arms, into her life.

And if that thought alone wasn't enough to terrify her, nothing ever would.

"You're not making sense, but if you want an hour, you've got it. I'm not sure about the credit, but you don't have to smile or be polite, not to me. Like I said, they won't be expecting us until about six, we've got plenty of time. So…you want to go inside, or do we do our talking out here?"

"I thought you were leaving."

"Did you hear a word I said?"

"I tried not to, but a few got through, anyway. Something about a family cookout and giving me an hour?"

"Annie, what the hell ails you?"

"Not a single thing." A dozen things, but no single

thing. "I'm just the way I've always been. About one glove short of a pair, according to Bernie. She used to work in a department store in ladies' accessories. Come on inside, I'll make us some tea."

With a look of pained resignation, Tucker followed her inside. He left the front door open, whether in deference to the springlike weather, or in case he needed to make a hasty exit, Annie didn't ask.

She dropped her briefcase on the floor beside the umbrella stand, stepped out of her platform shoes and shed the tan trench coat she'd worn because the day had started out cool and cloudy. Ignoring Tucker, she stood before the hall mirror, removed the pins from her chignon and dug her fingers into her scalp.

He watched her, a look of growing concern on his face. "Annie? You're not acting like yourself, are you feeling all right?"

"Better by the minute now that I've decided to take possession of my life again."

Leaning against the arched opening that led to the front parlor, Tucker crossed his arms over his chest and watched her. It was plain that he thought she'd lost her mind.

"I haven't, not really. Lost my mind, that is. Tucker, would you please put the kettle on? I want to splash cold water on my face and change out of my school clothes."

"Right, you do that."

Something weird was going on here. Tucker didn't want to think it was his fault, on account of last night, but this wasn't the Annie he had come to know. The old Annie would no more step out of her shoes and take her hair down in the front hall than she would undress in a public place.

Which she had done, he reminded himself. Maybe not in public, but in a strange house in the middle of a strange neighborhood, in front of a man who was little more than a stranger.

Funny thing, though…she didn't feel like a stranger.

There were dishes on the counters, the remnants of a pan of cocoa, cold and scummy, on the range. The toaster was pulled away from the wall, and there was one slice of cold, burned toast lying beside it.

Something was definitely wrong here. The Annie he knew was no neatness freak, but it wasn't like her to go off and leave things in this big a mess. Even he knew better than to invite mice, ants and roaches.

She'd said to put on the kettle. That meant tea, not coffee. He looked around for the coffee maker, found it half-full, with wet dregs spilling over the side of the basket, shook his head, then rolled up his sleeves and set to work. Whatever was bugging her, a dirty house didn't help. He'd learned that much the hard way, after Shelly had waltzed off with the eight-room, rock-and-redwood house and most of his liquid assets, leaving him with barely enough left to rent the dump he was living in.

Annie came downstairs some twenty minutes later, her face pale and her eyes shadowed. She'd pulled her hair back, fastened it with a rubber band, and changed into a shapeless khaki jumper and a white long-sleeved sweater. If she thought she could turn him off by dressing like a frump, she was in for a surprise. He happened to know that underneath all those shapeless layers there was a body so delicate he was almost afraid to touch it, but so damned tempting he couldn't help himself.

Behind all that pale composure there was a passionate woman who was just beginning to discover what sex was all about. One who was stronger than she looked, but who'd been restrained far too long.

What Annie needed, Tucker told himself, was a mature, patient man to help her shed all that unhealthy restraint, not some immature jerk like what's-his-name.

Glancing up from the sink into which he'd run hot, sudsy water to cover the dirty dishes, he said, ''What happened to your company?''

Not quite meeting his eyes, she reached for the tea caddy. ''English breakfast, wild strawberry or Earl Grey?''

''Your choice,'' he said, knowing it would probably be better than her coffee. ''I thought what's-his-name and his mama were still here.'' He knew better than that. Bernie had said they'd be leaving today.

''They left this morning. Eddie's coming back, probably tonight.''

''You haven't told him yet?''

''Told him what?'' She ran hot water into a stoneware pot and dried her hands on a crumpled linen towel. ''That I had a one-night stand?''

"Dammit, don't call it that!" Furious, Tucker grabbed her by the shoulders with wet sudsy hands. "That's not how it was, and you damned well know it!"

"Stop cursing. You do it too much. I don't do it enough, but it's not going to help, in any case."

"No? Then tell me something, Miss Prim-and-Proper Assistant Principal, what's it going to take to get us out of this mess we're in?"

"Define *mess.*" Voice calm, eyebrows slightly elevated. The old Annie was back. Cool, controlled, using her ladylike arrogance to cover a deep well of insecurity.

"It's not going to work, honey, I'm onto you now," he said with a sweetly intimidating smile. Two could play at this game.

"The kettle's beginning to steam, I have to make the tea."

"No you don't. I've lived a long, healthy life without ever drinking the stuff. Now, tell me what's going on with you, Annie, and don't forget—I've got ways of making you talk."

"Don't try to sound like Humphry Bogart, it won't work."

"That was my Clint Eastwood. Listen, Annie, we've got to come to terms with this—with whatever it is that's going on between us. Now, I can go first if it'll help."

"Thanks, I appreciate it. Close the door on your way out, will you?"

"You know what? You've got a smart mouth, lady."

"I try."

"Too bad for you, mine's smarter."

What could he do? He had to prove it. The tea was forgotten. The kettle continued to steam until, with one hand, Tucker reached over and switched off the burner.

"Ah, Annie, what am I going to do with you," he groaned after kissing her until neither of them could stand unassisted.

Leaning against the counter, Annie was gasping for breath, her headache forgotten. Tucker's arms were around her waist, holding her in a way that left her in no doubt as to his condition.

He was dangerously aroused.

So was she. Her breasts throbbed. She throbbed all over. "Technically, it wouldn't be a one-night stand if we, um—did it again, would it?"

"No, ma'am. Technically, it probably wouldn't."

"Although it's midafternoon, and that wouldn't count, would it?"

"Let's not play the semantics game, okay? Annie, where's your bedroom?"

"Upstairs."

"Don't you have a bed closer than that?"

She took a deep breath, struggling to regain her composure. "Maybe we'd better talk it over first."

"We'll talk later, I promise. Come on, I can make it up one flight of stairs if you'll hold on to me."

They made it together. Tucker never released his

grip on her waist. His hand spread over her hipbone, caressing, sliding the layers of clothing over her sensitive skin. Halfway up, when they came to the landing, he turned her in his arms and covered her eager mouth with his. Then he kissed her throat, her eyes, the side of her nose. It was as if he couldn't get enough of her.

With trembling hands Annie tugged his shirt loose and slid her hands up over his naked body, thrilling to the way he gasped when her fingertips brushed over his nipples.

"Yours react the same as mine," she marveled. "I never knew that." She touched him again and learned that his body was as hungry for her touch as hers was for his.

They were still on the stair landing. She was still wearing a pullover sweater under her jumper and another layer under that. She throbbed. Every beat of her heart was echoed in that incredibly sensitive place between her legs. She wanted his hand there, his mouth, his—

She wanted him....

"Hurry," she said hoarsely when he tore his mouth away from hers to gasp for air. "It's not far."

"I don't think—"

"Don't try. Tucker, let's not talk about it, let's *do* it."

He laughed, a broken sound, and said, "Catch you on a stair landing and you're something else." Together they stumbled up the last four steps and turned into the door on the right. Her room was old-fashioned because she'd never seen any reason to re-decorate. The bed was a double, but at this point nei-ther of them would have cared if it had been a single cot.

Tucker, fully clothed, but with his shirt unbuttoned, lay down and drew her down on top of him. Burying his face in her throat, he murmured, "I love the way you smell—the way you taste."

So much for all those alluring perfume ads. Evi-dently castile soap and unscented shampoo worked just as well. "Me, too, you." He tasted clean and musky and masculine. There was nothing at all arti-ficial about the scent of his warm flesh. While his lips moved over her throat, his hands cupped her breasts, hardening her nipples until they tingled. She moved against the hard ridge of his arousal, needing to be closer. Needing to ease this pounding urgency inside her.

"Tucker—I can't undress unless—you let me up."

"Not an option." His hands slid up under her skirt and he went to work on her panty hose. Together they managed to remove his jeans and briefs. There'd been a time when she'd have been horrified at the thought of making love half-clothed, but this was Tucker. She loved him so desperately that clothes made no differ-ence at all. She simply wanted him. Now, and for as long as she could have him.

She loved him?

The days were rapidly growing longer. The sun was just sinking behind the treetops when Annie opened her eyes, yawned and rolled out from under Tucker's heavy arm. He didn't snore. How could a man sleep on his back and not snore?

Control. And she'd thought she was disciplined.

"Tucker, wake up." She placed a hand on his shoulder to shake him, and lingered there to stroke his satiny skin. Even when he was sleeping his muscles were hard as steel.

Satin-covered steel. So *that* was where that old cliché had come from, she mused.

Merciful heavens, they had done it three times, and it wasn't even night yet. Remembering the second time, when she had insisted on exploring every inch of his body first, she could feel her face begin to burn.

"Tucker? Are you awake?"

"Five minutes, hmm? Wunnerful dream…in bed with Annie, and she's…" He opened his eyes. "Annie?"

And then he closed them again and smiled a smile that was so smug she didn't know whether to smack him or take a bow.

"It wasn't a dream, was it?" he murmured.

"What if I told you it was?"

"No way. I know my Annie. She might piss me off now and then, but she'd never lie to me."

"You have a vulgar mouth, Tucker Dennis, did you know that?"

The grin widened. "Yeah, and you love it. Admit it, sugar, you came apart in my arms every time. What was it, twice? Three times?"

"Hush, I don't want to talk about it."

"I do. I like talking about it when I'm too bushed to do it again, but I reckon we'd better shove off pretty soon if we don't want the family to get worried and come after us."

The smell of hickory smoke met them half a mile away from Tucker's small frame house in the hills of northern Forsyth County. Harold was grilling, Bernie and Jay were in the living room watching a video on fly casting. Bernie thought she'd like to give it a try, as she was always open to new experiences.

"Where's the ice cream?" Harold called out before they'd even reached the front porch.

"Sorry, it slipped my mind."

"Aww, son—you must be getting old. They say short-term memory goes first."

Tucker slipped a quick grin to Annie. The only thing wrong with his short-term memory was that it was selective. Given the choice of dwelling on sex or ice cream, there was no contest.

Harold expertly flipped a burger and moved it to the cooler side of the grill. "Shelly called."

Tucker stopped short. "Trouble? What did she want? I've still got a couple of days."

Bernie appeared in the doorway, wearing blue jeans and one of Harold's raunchy T-shirts with big dangling earrings. "Harold was up to his elbows in raw hamburger, so I answered the phone. I thought it might be Annie with a bunch of excuses why she couldn't come, but it was that woman. I told her

Tucker wasn't home, so she wanted to talk to Jay, but first I put in my two cents' worth.''

Tucker groaned.

"I'm too old to stand on ceremony. Besides, it's all that woman's fault. This fellow she's going to marry? You might as well know, I talked to him, too.'' Hands planted on her generous hips, she assumed an indignant expression. ''Well, somebody's got to look after that boy's interests, and I've always been one for plain speaking. Man's got two grown kids of his own, but he don't mind taking on one more. I told him I was the boy's grandma, and if he didn't want him, I'd keep him, and he could just tell that woman I said so.''

"Bernie, why don't you let Tucker get in the house and sit down before you load him up with all this business?'' Harold gestured to his bride with the spatula. ''All heart, that's what she is. Wants to solve all the world's woes, don't you, sugar pie?''

"Annie, what do you think?'' Bernie demanded. "If you were going to take on a new husband and didn't want to muddy the waters, would you keep your menfolk apart until after the deed was done, in case they took a dislike to one another?''

Annie opened her mouth to speak, but Bernie was on a roll.

"That's what Jay's mama did. She's got her this big fish on the hook and don't want to take any chances, but I made her put him on the line and I told him what for, didn't I, Jay?'' Tucker's son had wandered outside, looking a bit sheepish. Bernie snorted

and said, "Fishing talk. Comes from listening to the
boy brag about all those trout he caught up in Colorado. Anyhow, they talked some, Jay and this other
feller, and come to find out, he's some hotshot sports-
man himself—owns a baseball team. Sport's sport.
Not all that much difference in fishing and baseball,
is there, Jaybird?"

"You got a lot to learn, Grandma."

Tucker stepped up onto the porch, still holding Annie's hand. "Jay?"

"Aw, I guess it won't be so bad. He's better than
most of the guys Mom hangs out with, anyhow. Man,
aren't those burgers done yet? I'm starving!"

After a late supper, to which neither one of them
managed to do justice, Annie and Tucker left Jay with
his grandparents and drove back to Annie's house.
When there was no sign of Eddie, Annie dialed
Rosa's number while Tucker headed for the kitchen
to put on a pot of coffee.

"Is he there?" Annie asked. "I really need to talk
to him, Mrs. Robertson."

"He dropped me off and went to see Donna. She
left a message on my machine saying she was coming
back early from her sister's."

"I see." She didn't, not really, but she was beginning to think there was more going on in Eddie's life
than she'd suspected.

"She was with him over there, you know. Her and
her girlfriend Stephanie. The three of them went all
over together."

"Oh. Well...I really don't know what to say, but I'd like to talk to Eddie if at all possible. If you could tell me what time he left your house, or whether or not he's coming back to Winston tonight?"

"I don't know about that. If I was you, I wouldn't be looking for him anytime soon."

Annie hung up and stared down at the phone for several moments. The old Annie would have followed the letter of the law, officially ending her engagement before getting involved with another man.

The new Annie hadn't had time to think. Events had swept over her like a tidal wave. Before she realized what was happening to her, she'd been way out of her depth.

"Well," she said decisively. "I don't really know quite what to do now. I guess I'll just do nothing and let nature take its course."

"Sounds like a plan," Tucker said amiably.

Tucker admired the long lines of Annie's body as she leaned forward to wrap her arms around her bent knees. *Elegant* was the word that came to mind. He'd never truly appreciated the quality before.

Eddie had come trailing in at half past eleven, just as Tucker was leaving, the night before. He'd wanted to stay, but Annie had clearly wanted to settle things with her former fiancé in private.

He'd left them to it, but not before staking his claim by telling Annie he'd meet her after work the next afternoon, as he had something he wanted to show her.

He'd brought her out to the development. Or rather, his favorite part of it, which was yet to be developed, and might even have to be sold at a loss because it wouldn't perk for more than one two-bedroom dwelling.

Now he reached out to remove a twig that had caught in her hair as they climbed the wooded hillside overlooking the pond.

"The summer solstice isn't until June 21, but I can tell the difference even now," Annie said in that quiet, slightly husky voice that made all other women sound shrill.

Tucker cleared his throat. "Speaking of June, how do you feel about June weddings?"

"You mean Shelly and her baseball magnate?"

"I mean a certain house builder and a certain assistant principal."

Annie inhaled the wrong way and strangled. Tucker whacked her between the shoulder blades. "You need mouth to mouth? I can do CPR, too," he said worriedly.

"No, please." She blotted her streaming eyes. "Sorry," she gasped when she could speak again. "Did you say—?"

"Maybe I didn't make it plain enough. We both know I'll never be able to match your vocabulary."

"Tucker, for heaven's sake, was that a proposal or a rhetorical question?"

"There, you see? Here I bring you to my favorite place and try to act romantic, picking the briars out of your hair and tramping down the poison ivy so it won't get on your legs, and what do you do? You go trying to confuse the issue with all these big words.''

She flopped back on the carpet of brown leaves and covered her eyes with an arm. And then she began to laugh. ''I did no such thing. Besides, any time you want to impress me with your engineering terms, just start talking about sines and squares and logarithms. I promise you, my eyes will glaze over.''

''I don't want to talk shop, yours or mine, I want to talk weddings.''

She uncovered her eyes and stared up at him. ''Tucker, just because Shelly's getting married again—just because Harold and Bernie are flaunting their newlywed status, that doesn't mean—''

''Yeah, I know, but what if I said I loved you?''

For the longest moment she couldn't think of what to say, so she continued to gaze up at him. Up at the blunt, honest face of a blunt, honest man. After a while she said, ''I think I'd have to believe you.''

''You would? Why? That's one of those rhetorical questions, so you don't have to answer if you don't want to,'' he added hastily.

''Well, for one thing, it wouldn't be fair for love to be so one-sided. You said yourself there's something between us. I'm pretty sure it's love. At least, it is on my part, not that I have all that much experience.''

He nodded, a look of cautious joy filling his eyes. ''We're not kids any longer.''

''I know,'' she said soberly.

''Is your heart beating too fast?''

"Way too fast."

"Are you having trouble catching your breath?"

"Mmm, hmm. You, too?"

"Oh, yeah. All of the above. So what d'you think it means?"

"We've already had our one-night stand. We're up to what, four? Five? So it can't be simple lust."

"You're probably right. Lust wears off, or so I've been told, which means—"

"Which means this could be something a lot more serious." He stretched out beside her on the thick cushion of leaves.

Annie turned to face him, touching his face, running her fingers through his shaggy, silver-tipped hair. The spicy scent of the winter just past and the spring that was just beginning was all around them. "A whole lot more serious."

"Jay's a big responsibility."

"Jay and I get along just fine. He's promised to help me locate Zen before he leaves for school."

"You know what my house is like. I don't even own it, I'm only renting."

"There's mine, but it's more of a liability than an asset."

"Harold's good at repairs."

"Do you suppose Harold and Bernie would be interested—?" She let it hang there.

"In that case, you and I could— How would you feel about building right here? Our own woods, our own section of the pond? I could swing it by cashing in a few bonds."

"I have some savings. I'd been meaning to use it on roof repairs."

Tucker's face was so close she could see the shards of gold in his eyes, the growing flush on his weathered cheeks. There was definitely something going on in the area just below his belt.

Annie began to chuckle. "Tucker, would you just listen to us? Here you've just proposed to me, and we're talking about bonds and roof repairs. I guess that means it's love and not lust."

"Don't be too sure," he said, his eyes taking on a familiar gleam.

And then he went on to prove his point.

*   *   *   *   *

Silhouette Stars

Born this Month

Jerry Hall, Tom Cruise, Tom Stoppard,
Nancy Reagan, Ringo Starr, Barbara Cartland,
Harrison Ford, Linda Ronstadt.

Star of the Month

Cancer

An excellent year ahead in which progress can
be made in all areas of your life. There may be a
period of change in the autumn but don't be
fearful as the outcome will be better than you
could hope and you will see the necessity for
change. A lucky break in the second half of the
year could have you splashing out.

SILH/HR./0007a

Leo

You could find yourself pushing too hard to achieve what you want especially in your personal life. So try a little tact and diplomacy and the results could be better than you dreamed.

Virgo

Travel and romance are both well aspected and if linked you could look forward to an extra special month. Late in the month a friend needs a helping hand but be sure of their motives before offering too much.

 Libra

Energy levels are high and there is little you can't achieve. Holidays are well aspected especially those in groups. Career moves at the end of the month get you excited about the future.

Scorpio

Your ability to communicate constructively may help to bring about an improvement in your financial situation. This, in turn, will help you to build towards the future with renewed vigour.

 Sagittarius

Romance is in the air and you will feel in demand both with partners and friends, making this a social, easy going month with very little to trouble you, so enjoy!

Capricorn

A social month in which you may have to make unexpected journeys. Work opportunities will bring an added financial boost and you will realise your talents are being fully appreciated.

Aquarius

Your love life receives a boost and should become more meaningful than of late. As the month ends you may find your energy levels are getting low so take a break and pamper yourself back to full strength.

Pisces

You have a decisive quality to you this month giving you the courage to make the changes you have long desired to make. Be bold and you'll be amazed by what you can achieve.

 ## Aries

The lack of financial resource has become an area of conflict in your personal life. You need to sit down together and make an effective budget plan. By working in harmony your relationship will improve dramatically.

Taurus

As your confidence returns you will feel more positive and able to tackle life with enthusiasm. A lucky break mid-month gives you cause for a celebration.

  ## Gemini

Travel is never far from your thoughts especially the more adventurous kind and this month should see you planning another experience. A friend may want to join you but be sure they are as bold as you before you commit.

Look out for more
Silhouette Stars next month

❤™ SILHOUETTE
DESIRE ®

AVAILABLE FROM 21ST JULY 2000

FOREVER FLINT Barbara Boswell

Man of the Month

Cosmopolitan Ashlinn Carey was every man's dream, and after one passionate night Flint Paradise knew she was all he ever wanted. But then Ashlinn left. Now Flint was out to woo his city woman back into his arms…forever.

TEXAS MILLIONAIRE Dixie Browning

The Millionaire's Club

Hank Langley was the epitome of masculinity—and as rich as sin. Women threw themselves at him but none of them were quite right. Then Callie Riley started working for him and *everything* changed…

KISS YOUR PRINCE CHARMING Jennifer Greene

A sudden twist of fate turns Rachel Martin's neighbour Greg Stoner into the world's most desirable man. But going from friends to lovers is never easy, and Rachel knows she has a little coaxing to do…

THE SHEIKH'S SECRET Judith McWilliams

Being mistaken for his twin brother was OK. Falling in love with his brother's ex-fiancée *wasn't!* Yet Sheikh Hassan Rashid couldn't resist Kali Whitman's tempting sensuality. But would their love endure once Kali found out Hassan wasn't the man he claimed to be?

THE UNKNOWN MALONE Anne Eames

When Nicole Bedder turned up on Michael Malone's doorstep, he was certain she was there for a handout. But he soon found himself wondering what secrets the willowy beauty was hiding. Could he uncover the truth before he lost her forever?

TOO STUBBORN TO MARRY Cathie Linz

Marriage Makers

Ryan Knight was shocked when he caught up with old flame Courtney Delaney—how she'd changed! Gone was the wild temptress he'd once known! But he could see, deep in her eyes, the tiger dying to get out. How could Ryan unleash her?

AVAILABLE FROM 21ST JULY 2000

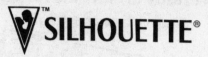

Sensation
Passionate, dramatic, thrilling romances

EVE'S WEDDING KNIGHT Kathleen Creighton
LONE WOLF'S LADY Beverly Barton
THE ICE MAN Brittany Young
I'LL REMEMBER YOU Barbara Ankrum
WIFE ON DEMAND Alexandra Sellers
ALMOST PERFECT Marilyn Tracy

Intrigue
Danger, deception and suspense

THE LITTLEST WITNESS Amanda Stevens
DREAM MAKER Charlotte Douglas
ONE TEXAS NIGHT Sylvie Kurtz
FOR HIS DAUGHTER Dani Sinclair

Special Edition
*Vivid, satisfying romances
full of family, life and love*

CELEBRATE THE CHILD Amy Frazier
THAT FIRST SPECIAL KISS Gina Wilkins
THE MOST ELIGIBLE MD Joan Elliott Pickart
FOREVER MINE Jennifer Mikels
THE BACHELOR KING Tracy Sinclair
THE BABY DUE DATE Teresa Carpenter

0007/22b

Get ready to enter the exclusive,
masculine world of...

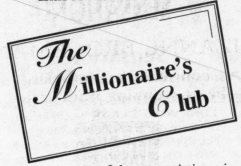

The
Millionaire's
Club

Desire's powerful new mini-series
features five wealthy bachelors—all
members of a very select, prestigious
club—who set out on a mission to
rescue a princess...and find true love!

August 2000
TEXAS MILLIONAIRE *Dixie Browning*

September 2000
CINDERELLA'S TYCOON *Caroline Cross*

October 2000
BILLIONAIRE BRIDEGROOM *Peggy Moreland*

November 2000
SECRET AGENT DAD *Metsy Hingle*

December 2000
LONE STAR PRINCE *Cindy Gerard*

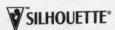